# Spirits, Beignets, and a Bayou Biker Gang

## Pyper Rayne Series, Book 3

by
Deanna Chase

# About This Book

It's date night! And medium Pyper Rayne is finally getting some alone time with her oh-so-sexy new boyfriend, Julius. But when a representative from the Witches' Council shows up during appetizers, the romance portion of the evening comes to a screeching halt. Julius is needed to deal with paranormal activity—on a cruise ship to the Caribbean.

An all-expense paid cruise to the Caribbean sounds like the perfect second date... until Pyper witnesses the death of a famous rock star. Suddenly Pyper and Julius are caught in the middle of a decade-old homicide. Now the race is on to solve the mystery or history is destined to repeat itself.

# Chapter 1

THE HARLEY RUMBLED to a stop as Julius pulled into a dirt parking lot. The scent of fresh rain mixed with musky swamp mud filled the early spring air. I hopped off the back and removed my helmet, shaking out my long dark hair. Directly in front of us, I spotted an old airboat tied to a dock on the bayou, and to the right there was a weathered shack with a sign that read: Swamp Witch.

"Friend of yours?" I asked my boyfriend, who just happened to be a witch himself.

He wrapped his arm around my shoulders and leaned in, kissing me on the temple. "Not yet, but if this witch has a cold soda in there somewhere, he or she is going to be my new BFF."

"BFF?" I laughed. "Since when have you joined the twenty-first century?"

"Since I hooked up with you." He grinned and tugged me toward the fuchsia-colored door.

Julius had lived his formative years back in the early nineteen hundreds. After his unfortunate demise at the hands of a fellow witch, he spent the next ninety or so years as a ghost. Luckily for both of us, he'd recently made his way back to the living with a little help from Bea, the former New Orleans coven leader. Now he worked for the Witches' Council, dealing with abnormal paranormal activity. But not this week. We were on an extended weekend getaway in Mayhem, Louisiana. The small bayou town was south of New Orleans and off the beaten path—perfect for riding the Harley and exploring places like the Swamp Witch.

"After you," Julius said, opening the door for me.

A bell that sounded suspiciously like a bamboo wind chime whispered through the sage-scented shop. I weaved my way through narrow aisles filled with herbs, chicken feet, incense, candles, and dusty bottles of potions until I came to a display of brightly colored voodoo dolls. I pointed at the purple one marked *Fire, Bacne, and Cauldron Bubble.*

"Bacne?" I said out loud and then chuckled, reaching for it. A voodoo doll to produce back acne was evil and hilarious all at the same time.

"I wouldn't touch that if I were you." A woman wearing a lime-green peasant skirt and formfitting tank strolled toward me. Her wide, honey-colored eyes crinkled at the corners as she sent me a welcoming smile. She inclined her head, indicating the voodoo dolls. "They're a little more potent than I'd expected."

"You're saying if I pick one up I might get voodoo'd?" I asked, snatching my hand back. A sharp pain stabbed me in the shoulder blades, and a glass jar smashed on the old wood floor right behind me. I turned, gasping out, "Oh no! I'm so sorry."

"It's all right. I can—No!"

I was already bending over to pick up the pieces of the shattered jar. But just before my fingers closed over the lid, the shop owner called, "*Purgamentum!*"

The pieces swirled up into a spiral and shot across the room, landing in a large waste basket.

I stood and wiped imaginary dust from my jeans. "Well, that was handy."

She was already headed toward the register area, shaking her head and muttering something unintelligible to herself.

Julius glanced between me and the witch, then cleared his throat as he followed her across the store. "Excuse me."

She glanced up, her brow furrowed. "Yes?"

"Can I pay for whatever it is my girlfriend just accidentally broke?" he asked, already reaching for his wallet.

"Oh no." She waved a hand and grabbed another empty mason jar from the shelf behind her. "That wouldn't be fair since it was Red's fault."

I glanced around the shop, seeing nothing but overcrowded shelves and dust particles floating in the sunlight.

"Red?" Julius asked.

She just smiled as she placed the unopened jar in the middle of the counter. Closing her eyes, she raised her hands and chanted in a language I didn't understand. Haitian, I guessed. A warm wind whistled eerily through the shop, raising the fine hairs on my arms. I glanced behind us, noting the flicker of the candles.

Julius slipped his arm around my waist, pulling me close as the wind intensified and whipped a strand of my dark hair over my eyes.

I clutched Julius's arm as the floor started to tremble while glass jars on the shelves rattled together. The door burst open, followed by all the wind being sucked out of the room. The door slammed shut, making me jump slightly as everything went silent.

"What—?" I clamped my mouth shut when red smoke materialized in front of us, curling and twisting into the empty jar still sitting on the counter.

The shop witch's eyes popped open, and she slowly lowered her arms, keeping them straight out and her palms flat as if she were forcing the smoke into the jar.

I stared, fascinated. The smoke coiled inside, resembling a rope, until it was all there, pulsing slightly inside the glass.

"*Fini!*" The witch slapped her hands down on the counter, and the lid flew up in the air, landing on the mason jar.

Julius and I stood there in awed silence, watching as it screwed itself on.

Julius finally nodded an acknowledgment at the shopkeeper. "Impressive. I assume Red is the spirit you trapped in the jar?"

She smiled. "Yes. He likes to play games when he gets bored. It's been quiet around here the past few days."

"Red is a spirit?" I asked, frowning. Why hadn't I picked up on that? Ever since I'd come into my medium abilities, the only spirits I'd encountered had been ones who had human form.

"A very old spirit. Not the kind you want to tangle with." She placed the jar behind her on a cluttered shelf. "Now, what can I do for you kind folks?"

As Julius enquired about a couple of cold drinks, I stared at the large jar and the red smoke swirling within. If I squinted and concentrated enough, I thought I might actually be able to identify the outline of a face. Pointed chin; sharp cheekbones; narrow, wide-set eyes.

"I wouldn't stare at him too long, child," the witch said. "He forms attachments, and then he's sort of hard to get rid of."

I tore my gaze from the jar and moved to the left, putting distance between myself and the jar. The last thing I needed was an unstable ghost following me around. Two weeks ago, when we'd been on the cruise ship *Illusion*, I'd had enough crazy to last a lifetime. Between the three ghosts trapped aboard and the certifiable witch who'd tried to turn me into his personal songstress, I was ready for a little normalcy. Well, as much normalcy as one could expect when she was a medium who was dating a witch.

Of course, that would be easier to do if we didn't insist on frequenting places like the Swamp Witch, which appeared more Voodoo than new age.

"Don't worry. He's not going anywhere for a while." The shopkeeper set a pair of ice-cold glass soda bottles on the counter. With a snap of her fingers, the tops popped right off and landed with a tinkling sound on the counter.

Julius picked his up and saluted her before downing half the beverage.

"Thanks," I said and took a small swig of cola, wondering if she was always this showy with her magic.

"No." She shook her head, holding my gaze. "Only when I sense my visitors have the gift."

I froze, my fingers tightening on the glass bottle. Had she just read my mind? Jade, the woman I basically considered my sister-in-law, was an empath and could read people's emotions. It wasn't much of a stretch to think there was someone out there who could hear thoughts too. "How did you…?"

A patient smile curved her lips and lit her amber eyes. "I'm a seer of sorts. Some call me the oracle, but I prefer Avrilla. Avrilla Chateau. Come." She crooked her finger as she moved out from behind the counter. "I just got in some fun things I think you'll like."

Julius and I shared a look as we followed Avrilla down one of the dusty aisles. When we got to the end, she picked up a lone bottle filled with green sludge. The murky contents looked like they'd been scooped right out of the swamp. She handed the bottle to Julius. "For when you need a helping hand."

He palmed the potion. "What's in it?"

She didn't answer. Instead, she turned to me, handing me a small dagger sheathed in a black leather case. "All this requires is a drop of blood to keep you safe."

The smooth mahogany handle had been polished to a shine while the black leather sheath had intricate carvings of cypress trees and swampland.

"Make sure you're ready for it when you use it. There's no going back," Avrilla said and moved to another aisle.

I glanced up at Julius, noting his eyes narrowed as he stared at the dagger in my hand. "What?"

"That dagger... It's really old."

"You think?" I held it up to the light and started to pull it out of the sheath.

He wrapped his hand around my wrist, stopping me. "Don't. Not here."

I frowned. "Why not?"

Julius shook his head. "Old daggers have a mind of their own sometimes. Be very careful about when and why you draw it."

"But how do I know if I should buy it unless I take a look at it?"

Julius chuckled. "When a witch handpicks something for

you, there's no question. Especially one who is a seer."

I shrugged. "Okay, but you know this a little strange, right? I mean, I'm not even a witch." Not really. A few weeks ago it was revealed that I might have a tiny bit of magic, but not enough to actually do anything with. Not on my own at least.

"Doesn't matter." Julius smiled at me and pulled me toward the checkout counter. "The items in this shop are spell-ready. You don't need to be a witch to activate their powers."

Well. Wasn't that handy? Most of the items in Bea's shop required magic, and thus someone with power, to activate them. Which, let's face it, was probably for the best since a large majority of her customers were French Quarter tourists. Only things like temporary love spells and mood enhancers worked for the average Joe.

"You'll want these too," the swamp witch said, placing a brown paper bag in the middle of the counter.

I leaned over, ready to peer into the bag. "May I?"

"Of course." The witch grinned, showing off her perfectly straight white teeth.

Inside, I found a pile of individually packaged voodoo dolls. The one on the top read: *Bubble, Bubble, Crotch Rot, and Trouble.* Another read: *Chafing of the Shrew.*

Glancing up, I burst out laughing. "Do these really curse people?"

She just smiled that knowing smile of hers. "Careful, they're potent. Especially *Impotent Gentleman of Verona.* That one can last for weeks."

Julius shuddered.

I laughed harder, imagining handing them out as souvenirs when we got back to New Orleans. "Oh man. These are evil in the best possible way."

Julius handed over his credit card and paid the bill without comment. I was still chuckling when we walked outside. Squinting into the sunlight, I followed Julius over to a picnic bench at the edge of the bayou.

I placed our purchases on the table as I sat next to him. "That was interesting."

"Not as interesting as that." He pointed behind the shop where the witch was standing near the water.

"Come here, Buffy," the witch called as she sat down on the dock, kicked off her shoes, and dangled her feet in the water.

"What the heck is she doing?" I asked, my skin crawling. There was no effing way anyone would catch me putting my feet in the bayou. Didn't she know there were snakes in that water? Poisonous ones. Of course she did. She was a swamp witch. Maybe she'd spelled them to stay away from her toes.

The water rippled with movement as a large alligator surfaced, heading straight for the witch.

I stood, my body taut and itching to flee. Which was fairly ridiculous since the gator wasn't anywhere near me.

Julius slipped his hand into mine and smiled at me. "Look," he said quietly.

The gator had climbed up onto the dock and laid her head in Avrilla's lap. The witch stroked Buffy's head, murmuring something to the large beast. Then she lifted one of the alligator's front legs and proceeded to trim its claws.

"Eww. Is she doing what I think she'd doing?" I asked, my eyes wide.

"For spells probably," Julius said and took a swig of his cola.

"Well... that's odd. And gross."

He chuckled, but I continued to stare, half expecting Buffy the gator to turn on the witch and eat her face off. But that didn't happen. When she was done, the witch stowed the collected claw clippings in her skirt pocket and waved the gator away. Buffy slipped back into the bayou and floated for a minute, then disappeared into the murky water.

The swamp witch waved on her way back into the shop. "Say hello to Sterling for me."

"Sterling?" I asked Julius.

He shrugged and held his hands up as if to say "no idea what she's talking about." When he finished off his cola, he stood. "Ready?"

I nodded, grabbed our bag of tricks, and followed him back to the Harley. After securing the loot in one of the saddlebags, I climbed on behind Julius and hung on.

Julius roared out of the parking lot. Half a block down the highway, he stopped at a deserted red light. He tapped his fingers impatiently on my thigh, waiting for the light to change. Only it didn't, and just when he revved the engine as if he was done waiting, the roar of another motorcycle came up from behind us.

A rider on an electric-green, custom chopper stopped beside us. He wore a skullcap helmet and full leathers with a double-headed snake on the back of his jacket.

Suddenly the noise of the motorcycles faded away, and the rider turned to me. He looked vaguely familiar, a snake tattoo crawling up his neck, but I couldn't place him.

"Hello, Pyper," he said, his voice gravelly.

Julius stared straight ahead as if he hadn't noticed the rider, and I instinctively knew I was dealing with a ghost rider.

Though I had no idea how he knew my name or why the motorcycle noise had faded.

"How did you do that?" I asked, waving a hand around us, indicating the silence.

"A gift from the swamp witch."

"Sterling," I said, understanding the witch's parting words.

His lips curved into a faint smile, then vanished as his expression durned deadly serious. "Your help is needed."

I stifled a sigh. Of course it was. It wasn't every day ghosts came upon a medium they could talk to. "What can I do for you?"

"Not for me," he said, his voice grave. "It's Mia. She's alive."

"Mia?" I asked, but as soon as I said the name, a young woman's smiling face flashed in my mind. The teen's picture had been plastered all over the news during a statewide manhunt when she went missing five years ago. She'd never been found and was presumed dead.

But thirty days after Mia Trebelle had gone missing from her New Orleans home, the state police had raided a shack out in the bayou that resulted in taking out her assumed abductor—Sterling Charles.

# Chapter 2

STARED AT the ghost, my mouth hanging open. Holy hell. My heart started to pound against my rib cage. Could it be true? Mia Trebelle was alive? "Where is she?"

He shook his head. "I don't know. I was tracking her abductor when the police cut my investigation short."

"But—"

"Twenty-three Motte Lane. Find—" His existence flickered in and out and back again, his mouth moving the entire time as if he didn't know it was happening, "—key—" Another fade out and back in. "—for answers."

"What?" I asked, biting my lip, but this time he disappeared with a pop and I knew he was gone. "Damn. Turn around!" I yelled and tapped on Julius's shoulder to get his attention.

Still sitting at the red light, he glanced back at me. "What?"

"Go back." I waved behind us. "I have to talk to the swamp witch."

He nodded once, and when the light finally changed, he turned around and whipped back into the parking lot. Once the roar of the motor died off, he asked, "Did you forget something?"

Shaking my head, I slipped off the bike. "Did you not see

the ghost rider?"

He raised both eyebrows in surprise. "You saw a ghost back there?"

I nodded. "He wants me to investigate a missing girl. He gave me an address and told me to find a key." After filling him in on Mia and what I could remember about Sterling's death, I added, "He knew who I was and mentioned something about the swamp witch. I think she sent him to me, and I want to know what else she might know."

"And why she isn't helping find Mia?" he said, getting straight to the point.

"Right."

"Let's find out." He slid off the bike and fell into step beside me.

It was then I took another good look at the Swamp Witch shop. What the...? I blinked, stunned by what I saw. The paint was no longer peeling, and the sign looked brand-new with a cute witch cartoon in the corner. "Holy cow. What happened to the weathered swamp shack? Did she just spell the place?"

He squinted, studying the building. "Looks like it. Though I think I liked it the other way. Much more authentic."

I had to agree. We made our way back into the shop, but as soon as I stepped through the door, I stopped in my tracks. Instead of the dusty, overcrowded shelves, the place was spotless, with neat rows of cutesy witch dolls, prepackaged tarot cards, carved candles, and neatly packaged herbs. Everything looked like it had been ordered out of a specialty catalog and was in no way authentic to the bayou.

"Hello?" I called out.

A short, perky blonde bounced out of one of the aisles, a

small stack of books in her hands. "Hello! Welcome to the Swamp Witch. Looking for something special?"

Julius and I shared a confused look. I cleared my throat. "Um, hi. We were here just a few minutes ago and Avrilla helped us. Is she here?"

"Avrilla?" Her smile faltered. "Sorry. I think there's been some confusion. I'm the only one who works here. Are you sure it was my shop?"

"Pretty sure," I muttered to myself and moved to the back of the store to peer out the window. The sun shone off the murky water, and as I stood there, a familiar gator crawled back up onto the dock. There was no doubt we were in the same place, only the store and the owner had changed. None of it made sense.

"Pyper?" Julius called.

I walked back over to him and the blond witch. She was perched on a stool behind the counter, watching me intently. I slipped my hand into Julius's just to ground myself in something real, because the shop and the blonde were officially freaking me out. "Sorry. Our mistake," I said and started to pull Julius toward the front door.

But as we moved away from the counter, I spotted a small container marked Alligator Claws. I paused, studying the gray plastic replicas.

"What is it?" Julius asked me.

"I don't—" My vision blurred. Then the dusty, dirty shop came back into focus and the claws turned into the real thing.

*Those are good for protection*, a voice whispered from behind me.

I spun, and the commercialized store full of slick packaged

items shifted back into place. *Crap!*

"Are you looking for anything in particular?" Bayou Barbie asked me.

I sighed, scooped up a handful of the plastic alligator claws, and dumped them on the counter. "I'll take these."

She took forever packaging them in cellophane, and by the time she finally ran my credit card, I was itching to get out of there. I felt like I was in the Disney version of a witch shop.

Once we were back outside, I blew out a breath. "That was…"

"Weird," Julius finished for me.

I stood at the motorcycle, staring back at the cheery building.

"It's not a spell," Julius said, standing just behind me. "I would've been able to feel it."

I turned my attention him. "No. Not a spell. At least not a normal one."

"What does that mean?" he asked, eyeing me in confusion. I had been told I had a small amount of power recently, like a teeny tiny amount, but nothing that would result in my sensing a spell.

I took a deep breath. "I think Avrilla is a ghost."

✧   ✧   ✧

WINDBLOWN AND MORE than a little unsettled, I strode into the Mayhem Bed and Breakfast, Julius behind me. The sound of my riding boots echoed over the glossy wooden floors as I made my way across the foyer to the grand staircase. I had my foot on the first step when a crash came from the formal living room.

"Hey are you—" Julius stopped mid-sentence, his eyes wide.

"What's going on?" I slipped around him, then clasped my hand over my mouth to stop the uncontrollable giggling. Moxie Mayfair, the inn owner, was bent over, frantically tossing a collection of brightly colored dildos, fur-lined handcuffs, and various tubes of lubricants into a plastic storage bin. And if that wasn't enough to kill anyone with embarrassment, the air-conditioning suddenly kicked on and the air from the nearby vent blew her short skirt up, flashing her ass cheeks, complete with a tattoo that said: *Bite me!*

"Oh my," I said before I could stop myself.

She stood up so fast she dropped her bin, and her collection of sex toys spilled out onto the fancy area rug.

"Your Jack Rabbit rolled under the chair," Julius said, his tone matter-of-fact.

I snorted and turned to him. "How do you know about those?"

He shrugged. "There are a lot of adult stores on Bourbon Street. I had a lot of time on my hands as a ghost."

Moxie's round face turned scarlet as she scrambled to collect her unmentionables. "Sorry. It's date night and I was… uh, you know… getting ready." She picked up a package of what I swear said Edible Intimates and shoved it behind her back.

"Maybe we should give her some privacy." Julius slipped his hand into mine and started pulling me from the room.

"Wait!" Moxie threw her fruity panties in the box and ran over to me. "Didn't you say you're a body painter?"

"Yeah." In addition to owning a café, I was also a body painter and sold photographs of my work at a local art shop.

She let out a relived sigh. "Great. Tonight is zombie night, and I'm going to need a little help with my costume."

"Um, I'm not exactly a makeup artist," I said, already backing away.

"Oh, I know. I want to do something special for Hale. And I think if I was painted to look like a zombie, he'd really go for that. You know, spice things up. His favorite show is *The Walking Dead*. A while ago, I ordered a starter kit for body painting, but I really have no artistic ability. And I thought…"

"You want me to paint you to look like a zombie so you can seduce your boyfriend?" I asked, my eyebrows raised.

She bit her lip and nodded, uncertainty flashing in her eyes. "That's crossing a line, right? I shouldn't have asked." Moxie started to back away, shaking her head. "Forget I said anything."

"Hell no, I won't forget," I said, laughing. "I think that's awesome. Of course I'll do it."

"You will?" Julius and Moxie asked at the same time.

"You bet your butt I will." I grinned at her. "Anything to keep the excitement alive in the bedroom… or living room," I added, nodding to the adult toy box.

She grinned, her face flushing again. "Thank you so much. I just know he's going to love this."

"Give me about twenty minutes to drop this stuff off and get changed."

Julius followed me up the grand staircase and unlocked the door to our room for me. "What about Mia?" he asked.

I set the bag from the Swamp Witch on the floor and immediately made a beeline to the chest of drawers. "I plan to pump her for information while I get her zombified."

"*Walking Dead* date night," Julius said, shaking his head. "That's a little…"

"Creepy?" I supplied.

"Disturbed." His gaze swept over my body as I discarded my leather halter top.

My lips curved into a smile, and I walked over to him wearing only my black lace bra and low-slung jeans. Placing my hand on his chest, I fisted his T-shirt and tugged him down so our lips were inches apart. "You don't want to role-play later?"

"Not if it involves you dressing up like a dead person."

I gave him a look of mock disappointment. "But I wanted you when you were dead."

His blue eyes flashed with a hint of mischief. "Correction. I'd prefer if our role-playing didn't resemble rotting dead people. But if you want to play the hot medium from Bourbon Street while I spell you with my magic…" He glanced down at himself and then ran a finger over the swell of my breast. "I think we can work something out."

I sucked in a small breath, ready to ditch Moxie and turn all my attention to Julius. He really did have a magic… ah… package. Only there was a woman being held against her will. And since Moxie had been born and raised in this town, she was sure to have details that would give me a good starting point. I took a step back before I let myself get lost in him. "Meet me for dinner in a couple of hours?"

He dropped my hand and nodded, not bothering to hide the mild disappointment in his eyes. "Bettie's Beignets, say six?"

The modest café was a half block down from the B and B. They served everything from deep-fried catfish to rum-soaked bread pudding. I'd do just about anything for more of that bread pudding. "Yep, I'll be there."

"Good. In the meantime, I'll do a little research of my

own." He pulled out his phone and started scrolling through his contacts.

"You're calling the council?" I asked, eyeing him. Julius had been a ghost for almost a century. His circle of contacts wasn't huge. Me, Jade, Kane, Bea, the New Orleans Coven, and the Witches' Council.

"After meeting Avrilla, I think it's wise."

"Good point." If we were dealing with any magical beings, it was best to be prepared. And after running into a ghost witch, anything was possible.

"I'm going to grab a coffee and enjoy some of this sunshine. See you later." Julius pressed a kiss to my temple and then strode out the door.

I sighed, realizing I'd just sent him away while I was half-naked. So much for a romantic weekend getaway. We had a kidnapping to solve.

# Chapter 3

"TAKE IT OFF," I ordered, mixing a bit of black and white paint to turn it light gray.

Moxie stood in the middle of her bedroom, wrapped in a terrycloth bathrobe, biting her lower lip.

"There's nothing to be embarrassed about," I soothed. "I've done this hundreds of times. Trust me. After I cover you with a base coat, you'll feel covered anyway."

"It's not that." Her face flushed. "Okay, normally it's not that. No one would accuse me of being modest. It's just…"

I put the brush down and gave her my full attention. "Just what?"

"Crap." She shook her head, her dark curls bouncing at her shoulders. Then she closed her eyes and untied her robe.

"Um, Moxie, is that a permanent tattoo?" I asked, trying and failing to keep the giggle out of my voice. Just below her belly button she had a pair of red lips with a tongue pointed down toward her lady bits.

"Oh gods. No!" She jerked the robe closed, her face turning even brighter red.

"Whew." I ran a hand over my forehead. "That's a relief, because imagine what that would look like when you're ninety."

She gave a tiny shudder. "Hale drew it on me this morning. Said he wanted me to be thinking about what he was going to do to me later."

"Wow. Hale appears to be a talented man." I grinned.

"Oh, he's very talented," she gushed, then clamped her mouth shut as her face turned scarlet. "I meant he's a talented tattoo artist."

I threw my head back and laughed. "Moxie, I think we're going to be great friends. Now lose the robe so we can get you ready for zombie night."

She stepped onto the old sheet we were using to protect her gorgeous wood floors, and then I got to work applying a base coat of color.

"So, besides *Walking Dead* night, what do y'all do for entertainment around here?" I asked, making conversation the way I always did with my models. Getting them talking about themselves was always a good way to loosen them up.

"Oh gosh. The inn keeps me busy most of the time." She rattled on about knitting and felting classes, online book clubs, adult toy parties, and something called Jamberry. But I started to pay attention when she mentioned an upcoming bike rally. "This weekend they all start rolling in, showing off their custom bikes, and man, the tattoos. I just love a sexy man with tattoos, don't you?"

"Sure. Who doesn't?" I said and applied another dab of paint to her rib cage. "Do local motorcycle clubs participate, or is it mostly out-of-towners?"

"I'm sure the Twin Forks will be there. They always do some sort of fund-raising for the local library."

"Twin Forks?" I eyed the work I'd done and longed for my

airbrush. It didn't look too bad, but if I'd had my regular supplies, she'd look like an extra ready for a walk-on role.

"They're from Forks Bend, a couple of towns over. Two brothers started it about ten years ago. Of course, it's just one brother now since Sterling went off the deep end." Her expression went dark, and sadness creeped into her normally bright eyes.

Jackpot. I put my paintbrush down and gave her a sympathetic look. "I heard about that. Did you know Mia?"

Her eyes went misty, and a single tear rolled down her cheek, making tracks in her freshly applied makeup. "Sorry," she said, dabbing at her face. "Mia and I grew up together. It's been five years, and I still feel like she could walk in the door any minute."

She would if I had anything to say about it. I grabbed Moxie's hand and squeezed gently. "I'm sorry. I didn't mean to open any wounds."

She shook her head and forced a small smile. "You didn't. It's just one of those things, you know? You're going about your day and then a memory or something pops up out of nowhere, causing you to blubber like an idiot."

"Not an idiot. And I know exactly what you mean. I lost my mom about ten years ago. There are still times when I reach for my phone to call her or I think I see her from the corner of my eye." Of course, I *had* seen her not too long ago, right after I'd acquired my medium abilities. That had been wonderful, but overwhelming. But she hadn't shown herself since, and I still wondered why. "The pain lessens, but we never stop missing them."

She sniffed and nodded. "It's just harder because of the way it happened, I guess."

"She just went missing one day?"

Moxie nodded. "Yes. She met Sterling for coffee at Bettie's Beignets, and that was the last time anyone saw her."

"That's terrible." I sat in the chair opposite her. "I heard he died in a police shoot-out."

She nodded. "Yes. They found him armed in the family camp out in the bayou. They thought he was holding her there, but when it was all over, she was nowhere to be found."

I was at a loss for words and about to get up to somehow comfort Moxie, but she squared her shoulders as a fierce conviction lit her eyes.

Then she said, "And you know the worst part?"

I shook my head. The only information I had about the kidnapping was what I remembered from the news, which wasn't much.

"Everyone thought he was the nicest guy. The kind who would give you the shirt off his back. He had a freakin' key to the inn for goddess' sake. We trusted him to watch over things when we were away. It's the kind of thing that shakes you to your very core." There was hatred in her eyes now. "If he wasn't already dead, I'd make it my life's mission to make him pay."

It was on the tip of my tongue to reveal that the culprit might not be Sterling, but I swallowed the urge, not wanting to say anything I couldn't prove. Instead, I picked up the tiny scraps of white fabric she'd laid on her bed and handed them to her. "I'm sorry about your friend. I can't even imagine."

She took the tiny skirt and strapless top and proceeded to put them on. "No one can."

I could though. I'd seen more in the past few years than

most had: black-magic users, demons, evil witches, and murders. None of it was pretty. And if there was anything I could do to help Mia Trebelle get home, I'd do it. "Can you tell me about her? What did she do for a living?"

Moxie's eyes narrowed, and her easy tone vanished. "What do you mean? What does it matter what she did for a living? Because I've had enough of people blaming her for the kidnapping. Just because she used to dance doesn't—"

"Gods no! I'm not blaming anyone." I held a hand up. "Not at all. I just thought you'd like to talk about your friend. You know, share your memories of her instead of what happened." Ultimately, even though I did want information about Mia and was now intensely curious what kind of dancing she'd done, what I really wanted at that moment was to see the spark of joy in Moxie's eyes again. Here she was, all zombified for a date night, and my questions had made her upset.

"Oh." A soft smile claimed Moxie's lips as her shoulders relaxed. "Mia was the kindest girl in town. She always had a smile on her face, an extra dollar to lend, and was fiercely loyal. If you were her friend, you were her friend for life." She glanced over at her chest of drawers and pointed to a pretty glass perfume bottle. "She made that for me after a particularly tough winter."

I glanced at the purple-and-blue iridescent bottle. "She was a glassblower?" I asked, surprised.

"What? Oh no. She made what's in the bottle. It's a potion to cure the flu. I'm one of those people who gets deathly ill every year. She made it as a preventative. I take one draught each year in early October, and I'm good through spring." She grabbed the bottle and studied it as she tilted it to the side.

"Well, I used to anyway. Last season I took the last of it."

"A healer then," I said, finally catching on. That meant she had at least some magic. That could be useful when trying to track her down.

"Yeah. An aspiring one anyway." She clutched the bottle, then very carefully put it down. "Or was."

And would be again, I vowed silently. Because right then and there, I decided I wasn't leaving Mayhem until Julius and I brought Mia home.

"She sounds like a special person," I said, placing a light hand on Moxie's arm.

The woman nodded, but this time when the tears formed in her eyes, she gave me a genuine smile too. "The best friend a girl could ever have actually. She's the reason Hale and I got together. She liked playing matchmaker."

"I bet she's thrilled you two are going strong." I waved at her zombified body and gave her a knowing smile. "Anyone who'd go through this much trouble for date night must be motivated."

Moxie snickered. "Yeah. Mia would approve."

✧   ✧   ✧

THE SWEET SCENT of rising dough combined with Cajun spices assaulted me as I strode into Bettie's Beignets. The worn old cypress-wood floors were discolored but had been recently refinished. The gleaming white walls appeared freshly painted as did the brightly colored tables and chairs. Someone had been updating. The old cottage sat on the edge of the bayou with a screened-in porch that overlooked the water. I loved everything about it, including the grizzly owner behind the bar.

"It's about time you showed. Your man's been waitin' for ya outside," he said to me, jerking his thumb toward the patio. "Any longer and we were gonna start chargin' 'im rent."

I waved an impatient hand. "Don't give me that. If I know Julius, he's already ordered three appetizers and a couple of drinks."

"We coulda put him at the bar fer that."

"Don't worry, Otis. We've got you covered on the tip." I smiled sweetly at him as I strode toward the porch.

"I'll have Boots bring you your sweet tea," he called after me, the perpetual scowl wiped from his grizzly mug.

"Sounds like you've got his number," Julius said and brushed a kiss over my cheek.

"He just wants someone to grump at who's not afraid to dish it back."

"No, he wants to flirt with a pretty woman."

I laughed. "That's flirting?"

"It is for a sixty-something-year-old man who hasn't had a woman in his life for a decade or more."

A pixie-like waitress appeared and dropped off my iced tea. "Can I get you something to eat?"

Julius ordered the savory crawfish beignets, and I went with the etouffee. Sweet potato fries, bread, and crab dip were already on the table. By the time we were done with dinner, Julius was going to need to roll me back to the inn. But not too early. I didn't want to walk in on zombie night. The image of Moxie and Hale stumbling toward each other with their mouths open made me giggle.

"What?" Julius asked, picking up his draft beer.

"It has to do with zombie date night. You don't want to

know." I grinned and grabbed a fry.

"You're right. I don't. But I have some information for you."

I set the fry down on the plate and gave him my full attention. "Tell me."

"Mia Trebelle was a seer. She knew about her impending abduction."

# Chapter 4

"**Y**OU'RE NOT SERIOUS?" I asked Julius, though judging by the pinched lines around his narrowed eyes, he was speaking the truth. "Is that what you learned from the council?"

He nodded. "They had one thin file on her. It appears she informed them of her vision just a week before she went missing. I checked in with Bea as well. She didn't know her at all."

Beatrice Kelton was the former New Orleans coven leader. If she didn't know anything about Mia, no one in the city did. I took a sip of my tea and reached for a piece of bread to settle the ache already forming in my gut. "The council knew and they did nothing?"

"No, not nothing. But her information was spotty at best. Just that she saw herself stuffed in the trunk of a blue, four-door car and then dragged out to a one-room bayou camp where she'd be forced into domestic slavery."

Jeez. That was horrific. Camps were what people called the cabins and shacks out on the bayou. They could be anything from a rotting one-room structure to a fancy bayou vacation house. "Let me guess, Sterling had a blue four-door."

"A 1982 Cadillac Seville. He'd been tinkering and talking

about restoring it."

"I guess it's easy to see why they pointed the finger at him. According to Moxie, he was the last person she was seen with as well. Was there any other connection between Mia and Sterling?"

"Not in the file. Because Mia was a swamp witch, not much is known about her when it comes to council business. It appears she went to them as a last resort."

"A lot of good that did her," I muttered. People who lived out in the swamps and bayous largely kept to themselves. That went for witches and Voodoo practitioners as well. It wasn't a surprise that Mia hadn't tried to hook up with the council or the New Orleans coven.

"I don't know what happened on the council's end. There's no follow-up at all."

My blood started to boil. This wasn't the first time the council waited until it was too late to actually do anything. "Isn't there some kind of protection spell? Or finding spell they could've done?"

"I'd think so." Julius drew his brows together. "But you know as well as I do that when it comes to magic, there's never a cut-and-dried solution."

I blew out a breath. He had a point. Magic was a living, breathing thing. Every witch had their own unique abilities, and no spell worked exactly the same on each person. Or so it seemed to me. After all the crap I'd seen over the past few years, it would be foolish to take anything for granted. "Do you think we could try a finding spell for Mia?"

Julius's eyes lit with interest, but the spark went out just as fast. "We don't have a connection to her. And even if we did, we'd be better off heading back to New Orleans where Jade could lead the spell at the coven circle. I just don't think it's something I can do on my own."

"Right." Jade had done at least one finding spell before, but that had been to find her biological father. She definitely had a connection to him. "Maybe if we check out that address Sterling gave us, we'll find something that belonged to her."

"Maybe," Julius said, but there was doubt in his tone, and with good reason. It *had* been five years since she'd gone missing.

"We can always try." The waitress arrived, placing our dinners in front of us. "After we eat," I added, already digging my spoon into the etouffee.

Julius chuckled, watching me shovel in the crawfish-and-rice concoction. I never had been one of those dainty salad eaters. Nope. I liked food. And dessert. There was a buttered rum bread pudding on the menu that had my name all over it.

"After," Julius agreed and picked up his fork.

❖   ❖   ❖

"THIS IS WHERE we're supposed to find the key?" I asked Julius as I stared at the nearly deserted parking lot. A red pickup sat near the weathered office. "At Mayhem Gator Tours?"

"Maybe it's inside?" Julius gave me a dubious look.

"I guess so."

"Hey." A young man stumbled out from behind the office building, holding a bottle in one hand and a cigarette in the other. "Can't you read? We closed up hours ago."

The light from a lone lamppost illuminated him. I squinted, taking in the lanky teenager. He had dark, wavy hair that fell into his eyes, and there was just something about the way he leaned one arm against the wall while he glared at us that felt vaguely familiar.

"I'm talking to you," he barked and then took a swig of the beer.

"Sorry." Julius patted the seat of the motorcycle. "Just needed to make an adjustment. We'll be on our way shortly."

The teenager opened his mouth to say something, but another teenager, a girl this time, poked her head around the building and called, "Bo? What's taking you so long? If you don't get your butt back here, Jimmy's going to smoke the last of the weed."

"He better not. Dammit. That bag is supposed to last till I get my next paycheck." Then, without another glance at us, Bo downed his beer and took off to presumably save the rest of his weed.

"Looks like we stumbled on the party," I said to Julius.

"A party we aren't welcome at. Come on." He handed me my helmet. "We'll come back in the morning, check things out when they're open."

"And take a tour?" I asked, embarrassed when the question came off sounding like an excited nine-year-old.

He chuckled. "Seriously? You want to pay someone to show you alligators?"

I shrugged. "Gators are cool, man. And the bayou is gorgeous. If we're checking the place out, we might as well really check it out, right?"

He wrapped his arm around my waist and pulled me in close. "I can think of plenty of other things I'd like to check out first."

I leaned in and gave him a slow, lingering kiss, one full of promise. But when I pulled away, I smiled up at him. "That might be the only action you get if we go back to the inn and walk in on zombie night."

"Zombie night." Julius grimaced. "Nothing like eating brains to get one in the mood."

I laughed as I put my helmet on. "Whatever gets them going, I guess."

A small shudder ran through Julius. He shook his head while climbing on the bike. "Some lines should never be crossed."

✧ ✧ ✧

"YOU READY FOR this?" I asked, my hand on the doorknob. We were standing on the porch of the Mayhem Bed and Breakfast, listening at the door.

"I'm sure whatever they're doing, they're doing it in the privacy of their own room." Julius's tone was matter-of-fact, but the look on his face implied he expected the worst.

He had every reason to. A person who collected sex toys and made herself up as a zombie for her man clearly wasn't conservative. "Just close your eyes. I'll make sure you get to the room with your virtue intact."

He eyed me for a second, then lifted one shoulder as if to say why not? Then he held his arm out to me and closed his eyes.

"Chicken," I said under my breath.

"There is nothing weak about self-preservation."

I chuckled and guided him into the quiet inn. The dimmed overhead lights were just enough to get us from the door to the stairs without much trouble. I scanned the adjacent living room area. "All clear."

Julius opened his eyes and glanced around. "Thank—Oh hell."

I turned, following his gaze toward the check-in desk. No one was there except an oversized cat that had appeared from nowhere and was on full alert. "What?"

Julius pointed at the desk, and then his body started shaking with silent laughter. "Now I've seen everything."

I took a step toward the desk, eyeing the cat as he raised his hackles. "Relax, Mr. Laveaux. We're not doing anything."

"No, but they were." Julius pointed at desk. "And judging by the condition of this distressed wood, someone might have the splinters to prove it."

I zeroed in on the body paint smudging the desk. My mouth dropped open, and then my cackle filled the room, startling Mr. Laveaux. He let out a kitty screech that was loud enough to wake the entire street before darting away under the stairs. "Oh my. Looks like zombie night was a hit."

A perfectly formed grayish-white zombie buttprint was stamped on the desk along with what appeared to be the shape of Moxie's body. There was a handprint on the wall next to the desk. And if that wasn't enough evidence that the pair had gotten busy right there in the entry, the two white scraps of fabric Moxie had worn were discarded behind the desk along with a pair of jeans and a paint-marked black T-shirt.

"I'm telling you, someone is going to have a hard time sitting down tomorrow," Julius said, still chuckling.

I grimaced. He was probably right. The desk wasn't a modern-day piece made to look distressed. It was rough, and the zombie paint had worked its way into the grain. The evidence would last for a while.

"Come on." Julius grabbed my hand. "Let's go before they come back for round two."

A pleased smile tugged at my lips. As ridiculous as zombie date night sounded, it was nice to know people who were obviously in love.

As we made our way up the stairs, the faint sounds of giggling came from the first floor.

Julius grabbed my hand and quickened his pace.

By the time we made it to our room, I was the one laughing.

"Hush, woman." He unlocked our door, and before I could slide in, he scooped me up and carried me over the threshold as if we'd just said our vows.

The thought sent a bolt of tingling happiness straight to my heart. I had no trouble seeing myself walking down the aisle with Julius waiting for me at the altar. Gazing up at my boyfriend, I felt a goofy smile claim my lips. There was no doubt I'd entered lovesick-puppy territory.

"Why are you looking at me like that?" Julius asked, his voice suddenly husky, all traces of playfulness gone.

I shook my head but said nothing, too afraid I'd blurt out words I wasn't ready to say.

"You look... happy," he said, caressing my cheek with his knuckles.

Something deep inside me shifted, and my gooey heart hardened just a little. "Is that so unusual?"

"No," he said quickly, shaking his head. "Not at all." He turned and gently lowered me to the bed. "That look though." The bed shifted as he sat beside me. "It was pure. Unguarded."

I lifted one shoulder in a half shrug. "I'm on vacation."

He eyed me and shook his head again.

"I'm not on vacation?" I asked just to needle him.

He ignored my question, placed one hand on my hip, and leaned down, brushing a kiss over my lips. "That look, Pyper, was like seeing inside you. I want more of that."

My breath got caught in my throat. I wanted that too. More than anything. But to let him see what was inside me, to bare my soul, would mean revealing how much I wanted to be with him and how much I wanted the white dress, the fancy cake, and to see Jade in a ridiculous bridesmaid dress. It was way too early in our relationship to be talking about forever.

He pulled back and gently touched my lips with his fingers. "I know that's hard for you."

"It's not—"

"Shh," he said gently. "Not now, my lovely girl. I want to show you exactly how much I want you." His hand slowly made its way up my hip and under my shirt to my bare skin. And just as he leaned down, once again bringing his lips to mine, a loud bang sounded from across the room.

We both bolted upright, only magic sparked at Julius's fingertips as he peered into the moonlit darkness. I hastily reached over and flipped the switch on the bedside lamp, flooding the room with light.

No one was there.

In the absence of anyone obvious, Julius jumped up from the bed and stalked over to where a large ornamental vase had shattered over the wood floor.

"That didn't just fall by itself," I said, stating the obvious.

"No. But it could've been a spell or a curse—"

"Or a ghost," I said. But as I got up to follow Julius, Mr. Laveaux shot out from behind the wreckage with something dark and limp hanging out of his mouth.

"Oh holy mother of crimson!" I cried and jumped up on the bed, pointing at the cat escaping the room through the barely opened door. We obviously hadn't gotten the dang thing closed all the way. "What the hell was that in his mouth?"

Julius calmly walked over to the door and shut it. "Looked like the cat went hunting."

I gave a small shudder. "If there are any mice in this room..."

"If there was, I gather there isn't now," Julius said, chuckling.

I glared at him.

"Well, that's one of the advantages of having a cat, right?" He knelt down and inspected the broken vase. "We're going to need to clean this up."

I let out an irritated sigh. Damn cat. Why couldn't he have interrupted zombie night instead? "I'll go search out a broom."

By the time I returned with a dustpan and hand broom I'd found in the hall closet, Julius already had the larger pieces of the vase in the room's garbage can.

"Any new critters?"

"Nope. All clear. Unless you count those gator claws and voodoo dolls you bought." He pointed to the paper bag of items we'd gotten at the Swamp Witch earlier in the day. It was on the floor near where the vase used to sit, exactly where I'd left it earlier.

"Nope. I don't," I said, relieved as I went to work sweeping up the remaining glass shards. Ghosts were one thing, but dealing with rodents was entirely another. If a mouse showed up in the middle of the night, all bets were off. Moxie's zombie night would definitely be over.

# Chapter 5

M Y ALARM WENT off before the butt crack of dawn, and I contemplated ignoring it completely. Hell, it wasn't even light out yet. "Whose stupid idea was this anyway?" I muttered as I rolled over and nudged Julius.

He let out an unintelligible sound and buried his head farther into the pillow.

Cripes. I needed coffee and a shower. Coffee first. Definitely. Thank the heavens there was a Keurig right there in the room because waiting wasn't an option. Not if we were going to get moving before noon. After I brewed the sweet Colombian nectar, I grabbed my robe and headed into the en suite bathroom.

Way too soon I was out of the shower and drying off when Julius shouted from the other room. "What the hell?"

I cinched my robe closed and ran into the bedroom only to stop dead in my tracks as my heart all but melted. Right in the middle of the bed was a white-and-gold-colored, fuzzy little shih tzu with her head down and her tail wagging, staring at Julius with her sweet puppy dog eyes.

"Who's your friend?" I asked, sitting on the edge of the bed and petting the precious little pup.

His eyes narrowed as he cast my new friend a glare. "That dog just licked my ass."

"Um… what?" I asked, chuckling.

"I was lying here, in that dream state where you're almost awake but not quite. Then I heard the door open and felt the bed move." He glanced up at me. "I thought it was you."

My gaze darted to the door. Sure enough, it was slightly ajar. I'd closed that last night, hadn't I? I'd have to let Moxie know it wasn't holding. When I turned my attention back to Julius, I let out a huff of laughter and asked, "You thought I licked your, um, backside? Come on, Julius. Does that sound like something I'd do?"

He raised one eyebrow.

"Never mind. Don't answer that. Why were your butt cheeks on display anyway? I mean, the dog didn't burrow under the covers, did she?"

He gave me a flat stare. "I lifted the covers, thinking it was you."

"Oh." I covered my mouth and then fell out laughing again, nearly rolling off the bed as the dog started yapping at him.

"Christ," he muttered and climbed out of the bed, doing nothing to conceal his hard, muscular body.

I sobered, my mouth suddenly going dry as I stared at his perfectly shaped backside. No wonder the dog had sampled it.

"Stop staring," Julius said without looking back at me.

"You've got to be kidding. If you're going to walk around flaunting it, I'm going to admire it."

He glanced over his shoulder at me, heat smoldering in his gaze. I thought for a second he was going to retreat back to the bed, but the dog started pawing at my hand and growling as if she wanted to play.

I smiled at the little troublemaker. Then to Julius I said, "Go shower. I'll find out who's in charge of this little bundle of mischief."

"Mischief. Right. More like pain in the—"

I help my hand up. "No disparaging her. You'll hurt her feelings." Grinning, I scooped the dog up and snuggled her as if she needed to be protected. The dog gave out a yelp of approval while Julius shook his head and disappeared into the bathroom.

"You're quite the little miss, aren't you?" I said, leaving her in the middle of the bed as I pulled on jeans and a tank top. She wagged her tail, then rolled over onto her back, showing me her belly. Well, who could resist that? After rubbing her tummy and cooing at her some more, I scooped her up, put her on the floor, and the pair of us headed downstairs with her at my heels.

"Anyone missing something?" I asked, descending the stairs.

Moxie stopped scrubbing the body paint off the desk and glanced up at me.

The dog barked, making her presence known.

Moxie's gaze shifted to my feet. "Stella! Are you getting into trouble again?"

The dog wiggled her butt, then shot straight into the living room and disappeared under the couch.

Moxie sighed and gave me an apologetic look. "Crazy dog. Did she wake you up?"

I shook my head. "We're headed out anyway. But she did manage to break into our room this morning. So did Mr. Laveaux. I swear I shut that door both times. You might want to take a look at the lock."

Moxie's smile fell. "Crap. Okay. I'll have Hale check it

again."

"Again?"

She nodded. "The last guests complained about it too, but Hale said it was fine. I'm really sorry about that."

I waved a hand. "It's all right. Who doesn't love waking up to an adorable puppy? Even if she is a little mischievous."

Someone behind me cleared his throat. I spun and spotted Julius, his cheeks stained pink. A chuckle bubbled out as I recalled his introduction to Stella.

"Good morning, Moxie," Julius said, ignoring me. "Have a good night?"

The inn owner let out a contented sigh. "The best, thank you."

Julius and I shared a knowing glance.

It was her turn to flush, but instead of averting her gaze, she grinned. "Zombie night ended with a bang, if you know what I mean."

I choked out a laugh.

"That's... Well, congrats," Julius said and grabbed my hand, tugging me out the front door.

✧   ✧   ✧

"IT'S TOO EARLY for this," I complained as I slid off the motorcycle and covered my mouth to hide my yawn. The one cup of coffee hadn't been nearly enough. And the excitement of puppy cuddles had long since worn off.

Julius secured our helmets to the bike, then nudged me toward the swamp-tour office. "You'll thank me when we're tucked away in the air-conditioning this afternoon while the heat index reaches hell levels."

He had a point. It was still spring in southern Louisiana but it was unseasonably warm with what felt like ninety-nine percent humidity. If we made it back in to town before a thunderstorm hit, we'd be lucky. "Yeah. Okay. But I want drinks with my air-conditioning."

"Done." His motorcycle boots clattered on the wooden steps as we entered the souvenir shop. Stuffed gators, along with creepy gator skulls and teeth, lined one wall.

"Morning," a man said from behind the counter. "Y'all got a reservation?"

I shook my head. "No. But if you have space on one of your airboats, we'd love to hop a ride."

The man rubbed at his weathered jaw and squinted at an appointment book. "Looks like Bo has a few openings in twenty minutes. Pay here."

Julius stepped up and handed over a wad of cash.

I scanned the makeshift office behind him. There was a desk with scattered paper, a computer, and a wall cabinet. Not much to search. Or much opportunity with the old guy manning the counter. "Is that a restroom back there?" I asked pointing to the door in the office.

"There are Port-O-Lets outside," the man grumbled without even looking up.

"Uh, actually I was hoping to wash my hands. If it isn't too much trouble—"

"Fine. Go on back, but be quick about it. I don't want everyone thinking it's the public piss pot."

Everyone? So far, Julius and I were the only other two people in the place. "Thank you." I leaned up to give Julius a quick kiss on his cheek, and when I did, I whispered, "Distract him when I come out."

Julius gave me a slight nod before turning to inspect the gator skulls. But I heard him mutter a spell under his breath. A faint glow covered his hands, then winked out before he turned and called to the employee, "Can you get that skull down for me."

As I was entering the employee bathroom, I passed the older man, who was singularly focused on Julius, his eyes slightly glazed. Julius had cast some sort of spell. Good, that would give me a little time.

I smiled to myself. It was nice having a resourceful man around. Poking my head out the door, I spotted the man on a short ladder, reaching for a large skull they'd secured to the wall. This was my one shot to search for the key. Careful to not make any noise, I hurried to the desk, pulled open the bottom drawer, and frowned at the stack of cigarettes and Red Bull. At least it was organized. The second drawer revealed reams of computer paper and a balance book. The third had a stack of pens and lots of alligator jerky. No key in sight.

Scanning the room, I locked eyes on the filing cabinet. Something had to be there, right? Wrong. While keeping an eye on Julius and the old man, I rummaged through the four drawers, but they were jam-packed full of files. Nothing.

The only place left to look was another small desk with a plastic storage container under it. I pulled the lid off and jumped back, stifling a yelp. Holy hell. There was a baby alligator in there. The gator lifted his head but made no effort to move. No wonder. He was sitting on a cool pack. Keeping gators cool made them lethargic. They must've brought him out for the tour.

I quickly placed the cover back on the container, and just as I started to head back toward the door to the shop, I heard Julius and the sales clerk heading my way. "Dammit," I muttered and hunched down, intending to keep a low profile until I made my way across the room.

"What are you doing in here?"

I quickly moved my hands to my shoelaces, pretending to retie them. Glancing up, I spotted the teenager from the night before, only he was sober this time, dressed in a polo shirt that had a gator emblem and the initials MGT stamped above it. "I just need to use the restroom."

He glanced at the bathroom, then the door to the gift shop, and frowned.

I was halfway across the room, not directly in line with either. Time to go. "I thought the door was that way." I pointed toward the empty wall and gave him my best airhead smile. "I'm directionally challenged."

"Uh-huh," the teen said, grabbing the container the alligator was housed in.

I popped up, waved, and strode back to Julius.

Julius handed the larger gator skull back to the shop clerk. "I think a smaller one is more appropriate for the house. We'll pick one up when we come back from the tour."

The older man scowled and said something about pain-in-the-ass tourists and deposited the skull on the counter. Clearly the spell had worn off.

"Anything?" Julius asked once we were out of earshot of the clerk.

I shook my head. "Nope. Nothing. Party boy showed up and almost caught me skulking around. If that happens again, he's going to catch on." I nodded at the teenager striding through the shop toward the back door.

"Looks like he managed to avoid a hangover."

"Ah, to be young and indestructible," I said.

Julius smiled down at me. "You're pretty resilient. Battling black-magic witches and deranged murderers and winning is a lot more impressive than surviving a night of beer."

A spark of pride warmed my insides. I had done those things and not only won but brought those jackholes down before they could hurt anyone else. I was pretty badass if I did say so myself.

"Your boat is leaving in two minutes," the old man said.

"Thank you, sir," Julius said and the pair of us made our way out the back door and down to the dock. Five other people were already waiting to get on the airboat.

"Good morning," the teenager said, an easy smile on his face. "I'm Bo, and I'll be your guide today. I grew up on this bayou and with more than a few of the gators. So don't worry, you're in good hands. I hope you all brought your cameras because there's a lot to see."

"Got the latest Nikon right here," a young brunette woman said, holding up a fancy digital camera. Two others held up theirs as well while I patted my pocket, looking for my phone. "Got it." I pulled the new iPhone out and waved it.

"You're not going to be able to get very good close-ups with that," the bubbly brunette said.

Her companion, an older woman with silver hair and appearing to be in her sixties or seventies, smiled at me. "You're speaking my language, young lady. This thing Velma is carting around weighs a ton and has way too many buttons. There's nothing wrong with a point-and-click version that will send my pictures straight to the IG."

"IG?" I glanced at Velma.

"Instagram. Mamaw has over twenty thousand followers. She calls herself the Blue-Haired Cajun and posts about everything she does. Baking pies, canning pickles, grooming her cat, deer huntin'. Just last week she posted about her Bible group skinny-dipping in the bayou. Bachelder's butt went viral. It was fantastic."

"I told him he should get that mole removed. No one should have a penis-shaped mole creepin' toward their anus. It just ain't right."

The other four people waiting started snickering.

"You are awesome," I exclaimed, holding my hand out to Velma's mamaw. "I'm Pyper, and this is my boyfriend Julius."

"Celia Kay," the woman said, shaking my hand. "But my friends call me Kitty."

"Nice to meet you, Miss Kitty."

She smiled at me, her thin lips stretching over her perfectly straight teeth. "You too, Pyper. Now, let's go meet some gators."

# Chapter 6

BO MANEUVERED THE airboat through the bayou like a boss. The kid clearly knew exactly where he was going as he weaved through the waterways, seeking out the wildlife. We saw no less than two dozen gators, one of which came right up to the boat, waiting for Bo to feed him his breakfast of raw chicken.

"The chicken trains them to come to the boat when we come through," Bo explained while holding the chicken wing near the boat to entice the gator to come closer.

"Man. He's a beauty," Velma exclaimed while taking picture after picture. "Mamaw, get closer so I can get a shot of you two together."

Miss Kitty didn't hesitate. She grabbed a piece of chicken and started to swing it over of the gator's head. "Here you go, little buddy," she cooed.

"Ma'am, no!" Bo leaped in front of her, nearly knocking her on her backside, but not before the gator lunged out of the water, snagged the chicken, and nearly took her hand off.

"Awesome!" Velma cried and pumped her fist in the air. "Check out the look on your face." She passed the camera to Miss Kitty.

"Hot damn! My fans are gonna love this."

"Ma'am, please stay back. You nearly got yourself killed." Bo's face had turned white, and there was a slight tremor in his tone.

I didn't blame him. My heart was still pounding after seeing the twelve-foot beast nearly jump right out of the water.

"Nah." She buffed her fingernails on her red T-shirt that read TROUBLE across the front in silver letters. "You didn't think this was my first rodeo with a swamp dog, did ya?"

Bo swallowed, then took a deep breath. "I'll have to ask you to take your seat now."

"Sure, sweetie. I got what I came for." She sat next to Velma and, with the elegance of Grace Kelly, slid on a pair of dark sunglasses.

Bo shook his head and climbed back into his captain's chair.

The alligator floated near the boat, eyeing us, no doubt wondering if there was more chicken. We sat there for a few more minutes while Bo educated us on the Twin Forks preserve. "It's been in the family for more than a hundred years. The gators know us and are mostly docile. If we're lucky, we'll find Buffy lounging on the dock of the family camp."

"Buffy?" I asked as the vision of Avrilla clipping a gator's nails flashed in my mind.

"She's been living around these parts for over twenty years. Old Uncle Steele taught her to respond to voice commands between her routine sunbathing on the dock and waiting patiently for her share of the chicken." He smiled then, his surly teenage expression morphing to one of easy humor. "Never seen anything like it. She's almost like a house pet except she's a nine-foot swamp beast who sometimes disappears for days at a time. No one knows where she goes. She's only ever been seen at the camp."

Interesting. Julius and I had seen her... with a ghost witch.

"Maybe she has a friend with benefits," Miss Kitty said. "And when she's gone, she's off getting her groove back."

Bo chuckled. "I certainly hope so." Then he fired up the airboat, turned it around, and we once again flew expertly through the water under the canopy of trees and Spanish moss. A few minutes later, Bo slowed the boat, inching it along. "See that?" He pointed toward a freshly painted cabin. "Look at the end of the dock."

Sure enough, there was another alligator lounging in the sun.

Velma stood and snapped yet more pictures as Miss Kitty photobombed her shots with peace signs and duck faces.

And as the boat drifted closer, the gator lifted her massive head and turned as if staring right at us.

"Watch this," Bo said, gliding the boat toward the dock.

Buffy lowered her head and closed her eyes.

When the boat gently bumped the dock, Bo called out, "Buffy, retreat."

The gator didn't move.

Bo reached into the cooler and pulled out a raw chicken wing. "Hungry?"

The gator opened her massive jaws and waited. Bo tossed the chicken right into her mouth. Her jaws clamped closed and she settled back down for nap time.

Bo laughed. "Buffy, we're coming ashore. Retreat."

The gator lumbered up on her feet, then slowly slipped into the water. She swam around the airboat, then disappeared beneath the brown surface.

"I need a Buffy. And a moat," Miss Kitty said. "A gator like her would keep that gossipy tramp Usinda from interrupting every time Hot Handyman comes over to… uh"—she glanced at Bo, her suggestive smirk vanishing—"to keep me… I mean my property… maintained."

Both of Bo's eyebrows rose as he stared at her, his mouth open.

I coughed to cover my laugh, then turned around and gave her two thumbs-up. "Way to go, Miss Kitty. Every woman deserves a hot handyman at least once in her life."

Her smirk reappeared. "He's my second."

Julius nudged me with his elbow.

"What?" I asked, eyeing him.

"Stop encouraging her."

"No way. It's been a little quiet since we left Ida May behind. I need someone to keep me entertained." I hadn't realized how much I'd missed the ghost's inappropriate comments since we'd taken off on our road trip. Miss Kitty was helping to fill the void.

He gave me a flat stare. "I'm not enough entertainment for you?"

I small smile tugged at my lips. "Different kind."

Miss Kitty let out a wolf whistle from behind us. "Sounds like you two could use a room. What do you say, Bo? Is there a bed in that cabin?"

Bo, who was busy tying the airboat to the dock, froze and stared at us like a deer in headlights.

"Oh hell." Julius jumped from the boat onto the dock, clearly trying to get as far away from the group as possible.

I laughed and patted Bo's arm as I followed Julius. "Don't worry, she's just going for shock value."

"She's doing a good job of it." Bo finished tying off the boat and joined Julius and me on the dock; then he frowned as he studied me. "Do I know you?"

"Nope," I said, deciding to not bring up the night before. The other passengers didn't need to know our guide had been partying less than twelve hours earlier. Besides, if Julius and I were going to continue searching for the key, it was best to keep a low profile. "Not unless you've spent time in New Orleans. I manage a café there."

He shook his head, his shaggy locks falling into his eyes. "No, ma'am. I was born and raised on this bayou. I'll probably die here too."

"There's nothing wrong with that… as long as it's what you want."

A shadow of uncertainty flashed in his dark blue eyes, but it disappeared just as fast and he nodded. "It is. Where else would I go?"

"You never know. It's a big world out there." I'd grown up in Baton Rouge and settled in New Orleans after college. I'd gone on a couple of trips. To Cancun right after I'd graduated, and a cruise that was more *Ghost Hunters* than vacation. But other than those two places, I was a Louisiana girl through and through, so I was no one to talk about broadening horizons. But there was something about his lack of enthusiasm that unsettled me. Last night this kid had been just another burned-out teenager, but this morning he was engaging and intelligent. And for some strange reason, I felt compelled to encourage the improved persona. "College is a really good way to test the waters. You got your eye on any out-of-state schools?"

He snorted. "Out of state? I can't even afford a local college. No. When I graduate next year, I'll be working full time here at the sanctuary and probably the local bar if I don't want to be homeless."

"Homeless? What about your parents?" I asked before I could stop myself. I'd always worked as a teenager myself, but there had never been any threat of being homeless, no matter how strapped my mother had been.

His expression clouded, and anger flashed in his blue eyes. "My parents are out of the picture. My mother died not long after I was born. And my jackass father took off a few years back and left me behind with Emerson Charles. But once school is over, Emerson says I'm on my own. It's when the foster-care checks run out." He shrugged as if none of that mattered, like it didn't bother him at all, but the hunched shoulders, defensive stance, and tough-guy act told a different story.

Well, wasn't that big of Mr. Charles. The jackass. What kind of person made it clear to a kid they only kept them around for the state checks? Soulless ones. My heart squeezed at the pain the kid was hiding beneath his tough façade. It was a wonder Bo was as put together as he was.

"I'm sorry. It was rude of me to pry." I wanted to say something about financial aid and scholarships, but I'd already crossed a line once. Who was I to try to guide him with major life decisions? I opened my mouth to say something anyway but was cut off by a familiar voice.

*Did someone summon me? I thought I heard something about someone missing me.*

Ida May. I'd know her anywhere. I turned slightly, spotting

her glancing around with a scowl on her face.

*What the hell balls are we doing out here in mosquito alley? I mean, I just got back and now I have to tromp around here in the swamp. Whose great idea was this?*

Behind me, I heard Julius mutter an oath under his breath, and I couldn't help chuckling. He also had the gift to see Ida May, much to his dismay. She was more than a handful most of the time.

"Something funny?" Bo asked, a hard edge suddenly coloring his tone.

"What? No. Sorry," I said, biting back a grimace. He'd thought I was laughing at him. "Not at all. I was just—"

"Never mind." He swept past me, heading toward the cabin with the rest of the group.

"What do you mean you just got back?" I asked Ida May as I turned around to find her hovering near Julius, her hands laced behind her back. Her dark curls were pulled back into a low ponytail, a new look for her. But she was still wearing black thigh-high stockings and a lacy sleeveless nightgown, her lady-of-Storyville outfit she'd perished in back in the early nineteen hundreds.

*I went on a little excursion up north. Saw an old friend. Now I'm back. That's all.*

The normal sass was missing in her tone, and if I didn't know better, I'd say she looked depressed. But that couldn't be the case. Ida May was never depressed. Irritated? Annoyed? Frustrated? Sure. She was all those thing. But never depressed. "What's wrong?"

She shook her head. *Nothing.*

"Doesn't look like nothing," I pressed, noting sadness in her expression. "You still upset about Bootlegger?"

She scoffed. *Gods no. What made you think about him?*

It had only been a couple of weeks since we'd been on the cruise ship, and she'd been determined to hook up with the pirate ghost. Only he'd had questionable morals, not that she seemed to particularly care about that, but in the end he'd reunited with his one true love. That was bound to make any ghost a little wistful. "Just wondering what's got you down."

*Returning to the café where no one can hear me. Talking to myself sucks.*

"Understandable."

*Whatever.* She waved a hand, dismissing the conversation. *Why are you two tromping around in the swamp?*

"We're looking for someone. Want to do me a favor?"

She nodded. *Sure. Want me to grab someone's butt? The young guy is pretty hot. I could—*

"No! Jeez. He's a minor."

She shrugged. *Whatever. Back in my day as long as they paid—*

"Ida May!" Cripes. You could take the ghost out of Storyville—New Orleans' red light district during the early nineteen hundreds—but you couldn't take the Storyville out of the ghost. "Hands off the kid."

*Fine. Party pooper. Want me to scare the crap out of them instead?*

"Just create a diversion. I need to search the cabin." I stared at the open door the rest of the group had disappeared through.

*I'm on it.*

"Are you sure that was a good idea?" Julius asked as we made our way up the cabin steps.

"No. But I'm certain it will be entertaining."

"I hope that's all it'll be," he said and held the door open for me.

Bo was standing in the middle of the room, explaining that the land and cabin had been in the family for over two hundred years, that up until forty years ago most of the family had been born right there in the cabin. I tuned him out and scanned the one room. The weathered wood floors had been refinished recently, but the paint on the walls was starting to peel. The kitchen in the back had old built-in cabinets and a vintage enameled sink.

The cabinets. I'd search those first. Then the coffee-table-style trunk in the main living area. I leaned into Julius. "You search the bedroom and the bathroom."

"Got it."

Before long I got antsy, shifting from foot to foot while Bo went on about recent upgrades to the cabin, and I started to wonder if Ida May was ever going to come through for us. She hadn't even entered the cabin. But then just as I was getting ready to give up on her, the door slammed open, crashing into the wall and startling everyone.

Bo sprang into action, instantly reaching into a closet and retrieving a rifle.

"Whoa," I said stepping back out of the way. Thank the goddess Ida May was an actual ghost.

"Trespassers," Bo ground out as he bolted by us, as if that explained everything.

"It's like the Wild West," Miss Kitty said, running after him, already taking pictures with her iPhone.

"Wait for me!" Velma flew out the door after her.

The other couple stood stock-still, their faces white.

"I'm sure it's nothing," I said, trying for the voice of reason.

"He had a gun," the woman said, clutching her husband's hand.

Crap. Now what?

"Um, Pyper?" Julius said, standing in the door, pointing outside. "You might want to see this."

I moved to his side and my mouth dropped open. Then I fell out laughing.

Buffy was in front of the house, running around in a perfect figure-eight configuration, with Ida May standing on her back, riding the gator like a surfboard. It was just too bad no one else could see her or hear her yelling, *Yeehaw!*

# Chapter 7

*RIDE 'EM, COWGIRL!* Ida May cried, pretending to hold on to reins. Then she glanced over at me, her eyes twinkling with her familiar mischief. *Hot damn, this is fun.*

She was somehow guiding Buffy through the front terrain, coaxing her to climb over driftwood and even managing to get the alligator to bat her eyes at Bo, who was desperately trying to get her back into the water and away from the guests.

"Buffy!" He scowled. "What has gotten into you?" The teenager grabbed his phone, took one look at it and cursed. "No signal. Does anyone have a working cell phone? We need to get a tranq dart out here if that gator doesn't calm down."

Neither Julius or I bothered to even look. Buffy wasn't going to attack anyone. Ida May had her under control.

"I have one bar." The other couple stepped forward, the woman holding out her phone. Her hand shook wildly, and I was actually surprised she didn't drop the phone into the tall grass.

Bo strode over and grabbed it, dialing quickly.

"My followers are going to lose their minds," Miss Kitty said, holding her iPhone perfectly still. "As soon as they see this video, I'm going viral!"

"Video?" Velma, who'd switched cameras and had just gotten done snapping at least a dozen shots, moved to stand next to her grandmother. She let out an audible gasp. "What the freak is that?"

"Clearly that gator is on something. I bet she got into a package of nose candy, if you know what I mean." Miss Kitty tapped her nose and gave her granddaughter a knowing look.

It wasn't uncommon to hear about drug runners using the swamps. Not that Buffy's behavior had anything to do with a found package of cocaine.

"No," Velma said. "I mean what is that on the video?" She pointed at Miss Kitty's iPhone. "It looks like... Oh em gee, is that a ghost riding that alligator?"

I stiffened. Had Ida May shown up in her video?

"Go now," Julius said into my ear. "Search for the key. This is the perfect distraction."

He was right. Miss Kitty and Velma were giddy and squealing about capturing a ghost on film while the other couple stood frozen, watching them in fascinated horror. Bo was still on the phone and scowling at all of them.

I turned and ran back into the cabin. Ida May had certainly come through with her distraction. I'd have to do something nice to thank her. What did a person get a ghost as a thank-you gift? If only I could find her a nice ghostly fireman. A single one. She'd like that.

It took me no time at all to search the bedroom and bathroom. There was nothing but the bare-bones essentials. A bed, linens, a couple of changes of clothes, and minimal toiletries. Back out in the main room, I headed straight for the trunk. Empty. The last stop was the kitchen pantry.

Jackpot.

A rack of keys hung inside the pantry door. Under each key was a label. The first three read: electric panel, boat shed, and storage locker. The fourth one, the only one with the key missing read: Bayou Charles.

What the heck did that mean? I whipped my phone out and snapped a picture. Then I slipped out the back door, noted the small electrical panel that ran to a generator and a small wooden storage shed, no taller than three feet high with a padlock on it. Mia Trebelle certainly wasn't living in that thing.

We weren't going to find her today. But at least we had a lead. Whatever Bayou Charles was, I was going to find out.

When I got back to the front of the cabin, I eyed the rotting shed sitting about ten feet from the dock. The door was wide open, and the structure appeared to not be in use anymore. I mentally scratched that off my list and turned my attention to the crazy still unfolding in front of me.

Buffy had moved back to the dock and was lying right in front of the airboat. Bo stood about three feet from the beast, poking her tail with the end of a shovel and yelling, "Go. Get. Move on."

The alligator gave him a bored expression and flicked her gaze to Ida May. The ghost stood next to her with one foot resting on the gator's back.

"She's holding her there. I swear it's like a circus act," Miss Kitty said, her voice full of glee.

Ida May cast me a glance and called out, *Can I go now? These people are giving me indigestion.*

I gave her the tiniest nod.

*Thank the swamp gods. This place is more depressing than a whorehouse full of overweight politicians trying to get it up after too much whiskey.*

Julius stifled a laugh.

Ida May removed her foot from Buffy's back and said, *Thanks, Buff. Appreciate the help.*

Buffy lifted her massive head, nodding once at Ida May. Then she snapped her jaws at Bo, who was still poking her with the dang shovel, right before she slipped back into the water. The gator disappeared almost immediately in the brown water.

"I can't believe that just happened!" Miss Kitty shoved her iPhone into Bo's face. "Look!"

He was too busy waving us over to pay her any attention. "We need to go. I've never seen a gator behave that way before, and I want everyone on the boat before she comes back."

"But—" Kitty started.

"Now, please ma'am," Bo said.

"Come on, Mamaw," Velma said, guiding her grandmother back onto the boat. "We've got to get back so we can start posting this stuff. Your fans are going to go crazytown."

Of course they were. She had video of a ghost surfing on an alligator. Miss Kitty was about to hit critical mass.

✧   ✧   ✧

"Looks like today was sort of a bust," I said, pushing my empty plate into the middle of the table. After our adventure out in the swamp, I'd been starving and we'd ended up back at Bettie's Beignets.

"Ida May was entertaining," he shot back. "It's not every day you see a lady of the night surfing on a gator."

I snickered. "She does keep things interesting. Though I do

wonder where she goes when she leaves us. Off eyeballing men in locker rooms, do you think?"

It was Julius's turn to snicker, then he sobered and a mild look of horror crept over his face. "That's not funny. Can you imagine the running commentary?"

"Heck, yes." I laughed. "And for once, that's something I'd love to see."

A small shudder rolled through him. "If she ever follows me to the gym, I'm blaming you. No doubt she's hovering around, taking notes right now."

I glanced around as if I expected to see the dark-haired ghost sitting at a nearby table with a pen in her hand. But the place was empty sans Otis, who was busy wiping down the bar.

"Can't you just see her? She'd be looking up the shorts of every guy in the place, trying to get a peek at his manhood." Julius sucked down the last quarter of his coffee.

I shook my head. "Nah. Not Ida May. She's seen more peen than a urologist. She'd be more likely to sit on their laps and ask them to help her with her pelvic thrust."

Julius sputtered, spraying a thin sheen of coffee over my plate.

"Enough of that, missy," Otis said, plunking another cup of coffee down in front of Julius. "This is a family place. We don't allow that kind of talk in here."

I eyed the grizzled old man, sending him a semiflirty smile that never failed to win him over. "Seriously, Otis? The place is empty. Don't tell me you never told an off-color joke before."

He scowled. "I know what you're up to. Batting your eyes won't get you anywhere. So you can just cut it out right now if you want to come back into my establishment. I already told you this is a family place. Keep it clean or keep out."

I dropped the smile and nodded solemnly. "I hear you. Sorry. We didn't mean to offend."

Otis nodded once. "Good. Now, do you need anything else? Dessert? Bread pudding?"

"Cheesecake to go?" I asked.

"Sure. Key lime or blueberry?"

"Key lime," Julius said.

"Blueberry," I added, watching him carefully. His face had gone red with anger as he'd chastised us, and although he was acting as if he hadn't just threatened to toss us out, his tight grip on the pen had turned his knuckles white, and there was a muscle pulsing in his neck. We'd really pushed his buttons.

Over a silly comment about Ida May? It hadn't even been that bad. Just a little bit of innuendo.

"Hey, Otis," Julius asked, his tone conversational.

"What?" the man asked without looking up.

"You know anything about Bayou Charles?"

Otis stuffed his pen in his pocket and gave Julius his full attention. He drew his brows together and frowned. "You mean the swamp land the Charleses own?"

"Is that different than the Twin Forks sanctuary?" I asked.

He nodded. "Emerson Charles owns it. He bought it a few years back. We all thought he was going to add it to the sanctuary, but turns out he just wanted to build himself a place out there."

"Really? Does he live out there? Seems a little cut off from civilization. No roads, just boat access, right?" Julius did a good job of appearing like an interested tourist. It was impressive considering Otis had just chastised us.

The proprietor nodded. "Yeah. Most of the time anyway. It's on the south side of their preserve. After that nasty business when that girl went missing, Emerson just wanted some privacy in a new place. There's no better place to find it than the bayou."

"I guessed that judging by the six dozen no trespassing signs we saw this morning," I said, an ache in my stomach forming. Did Emerson Charles have anything to do with Mia's disappearance? Had he and his brother both played a role in the kidnapping? We'd have to try to find out what went down with Emerson after the shoot-out at Sterling's cabin.

Otis nodded. "Don't ever head into unknown territory out there. You're likely to run into the live end of a shotgun. And around these parts, missing persons are rarely found."

Just like Mia Trebelle. We had to find Emerson's camp. There was no question in my mind that was the place to start.

"I think we'll stick to dry land," Julius said, handing Otis a couple of bills to cover our lunch.

Once the man had returned to his spot behind the bar, Julius stood and held his hand out to me. "Come on. I have a plan."

I slid out of the booth and raised one eyebrow. "And that would be?"

"How do you feel about purchasing a camp?"

"What?" I stared at him like he was crazy. "Does something about me scream outdoorsy? I've never even been tent camping. Hanging out in a swamp without air-conditioning sounds like torture."

He chuckled as he shook his head. "No, but I do think you might enjoy a little real estate shopping. You can't buy a camp without seeing it can you?"

The lightbulb went on and a slow, easy grin claimed my lips. Anyone looking to buy a camp would have reason to be out on the bayou. I just hoped there was something for sale somewhere near Charles's land. "Julius, you're a genius. Let the real estate window-shopping begin."

# Chapter 8

"IT'S CLOSED," I said, peering into the one real estate office in Mayhem. Damn small towns and their lack of any regular business hours.

"Of course it is. It's after noon." Julius dug around in one of the saddlebags and pulled out a strip of paper and a ballpoint pen. After jotting down the phone number plastered to the front door, he slid his phone out of his pocket and dialed.

I busied myself scanning the flyers taped to the window. Most were just pictures of random land without any identifying information, but there was one with promise. In the description it said it was adjacent to the Twin Forks preserve. I grabbed my phone and took a picture. If we did manage to get out on the water, it could be our alibi.

Julius ended his call and grinned. "You're not going to believe who the realtor is."

I turned to meet his amused gaze. "Who?"

"You'll see. We're meeting in a couple of hours at Potions," he said, referring to the microbrew pub on the outskirts of Mayhem.

I hurried to catch up with him as he made his way back over to the motorcycle. "I have to clean up first," I said, climbing onto the back of the bike.

He glanced over his shoulder at me, sweeping his gaze over my body. "I think I like you a little dirty."

That smile tugged at the corner of my lips again. "A shower isn't going to suddenly transform my entire personality."

"That's good news." He leaned back, covering my mouth with his as he gave me a searing kiss that left me breathless. And when he finally pulled away, he said, "As soon as I get you back to the inn, we're going to finish what we started."

Then, before I managed a response, the motorcycle rumbled to life and Julius hit the gas, shooting us off down the street.

✧　✧　✧

THE RIDE BACK to the inn was short. Less than ten minutes. The faint trace of coffee from Julius's kiss still lingered on my tongue, and the thought of stripping off his clothes, running my hands over his well-defined, muscular chest had me quite preoccupied. I had every intention of dragging him into the shower with me.

But the moment we set foot into the inn, all thoughts of alone time with Julius vanished. Instead, we were treated to a shouting match of epic proportions.

"I already told you I wasn't with anyone," Hale spat out from the living room as he dodged a flying pink dildo.

"You're lying!" Moxie stood under the arch that led from the entry into the main house, balancing her plastic bin of adult toys on her hip. She held a metal chain in her hand, swinging it around as if it were a piece of rope. There was something hanging off the end of it, something metal and... Holy hell. She was going to whip him with nipple clamps.

I cleared my throat, but neither of them heard me over the crash of the table lamp that Hale ran into as he kept an eye on his crazy girlfriend.

"This has never happened before," she said, her voice wobbly now with tears. "What am I supposed to think? Huh? You left this morning right before we were about to seal the deal. Got up and left me while I was naked and waiting, I might add. And now you're not interested after you've been gone all day. Since when are *you* not interested? Who were you with? That slut Bella Donna? Or was it Cindy Lou? Or both, you two-timing bastard?"

Hale's face turned a deep shade of maroon, but I didn't think it had anything to do with embarrassment or shame at being caught cheating. No, he was pissed. Beyond angry. "I already told you once I'm not cheating on you. I won't say it again."

Another dildo went flying, this time hitting him squarely in the forehead. He sputtered and stumbled back, tripping on the fallen lamp. He went down, taking the end table with him. Curse words flew out of his mouth faster than Mamaw's after someone swiped her moonshine stash.

"Ohmigod!" she cried and ran to his side. "I'm sorry. I didn't mean to peg you between the eyes. I mean, who knew that thing could be so aerodynamic?"

Hale ran his hand over his face and then gave her an incredulous look. "You threw that thing straight at my head. What were you expecting it to do?"

"I expected you to duck. Or are you too tired after your afternoon of grab-ass with goddess knows who?"

"That's it." Hale brushed her off, climbed to his feet, and

stormed out of the room. He kept his head down, not acknowledging us as he yanked the front door open and called back, "I'm going to Jake's house. Cross your fingers he doesn't make a pass at me since apparently I have no self-control!"

He finally glanced our way. "Sorry about the yelling." Then he slammed the door so hard the walls rattled, followed by an ornate wall clock crashing to the wood floor. Glass shattered and clock parts rolled under the desk.

"Uh…," I said and waved an arm at the mess. "Got a broom? We can help you clean this up."

"No, thanks." She sniffed and wiped at her eyes. "I'll get it. We just had a little argument."

Little? That was a slight understatement, I'd say. "What happened? I thought zombie night was a huge success?"

She nodded and reached into a hall closet to retrieve a broom. "It was. But then this morning he got a call from Emerson and just left even though I'd just done a striptease for him…. And this afternoon, he just said he wasn't interested."

"Emerson? Emerson Charles?" I asked.

She nodded and pushed back her dark curls. "Hale does odd jobs for him on the regular. Frankly, I'm getting a little tired of coming in second fiddle to that manwhore."

I raised one eyebrow.

Julius cleared his throat. "Maybe I should give you ladies some time to talk."

"No!" Moxie turned around and grabbed his arm as if she was going to physically force him to stay. "I think I need a man's perspective."

Julius gave me a panicked look, and I had to stifle the laugh bubbling to the surface.

"Please," Moxie begged, tears welling in her eyes again.

I took the broom from her and started sweeping, waiting to see what Julius would say.

Finally he closed his eyes and nodded. "All right. What seems to be the issue?"

"Well." She bit her lip. "When a man is *always* interested, and I do mean always, isn't it unusual to turn a girl down when she's offering to do *anything* you want?"

"Um…" Julius gave me a silent plea for help.

"Maybe he was just tired. You did say zombie night was a hit, right?" I bent down and scooped the remnants of the clock into a dustpan.

"Sure." Moxie plopped down on the bottom stair and rubbed at her temple. "But he's always been up for round two. Even round three. I just… I don't know. Something is off about him today. And I know what goes on over there at the Charles camp. They have biker babes there all the time. I think he's cheating on me. I just have that feeling."

"The Charles camp?" I asked. "You mean Emerson's place in the bayou?" Hadn't Otis said no one went out there?

"What? No. He has a place in Twin Forks with a huge garage where they all *supposedly* work on their motorcycles. Hale said he was there rebuilding a carburetor. But I don't believe him. He doesn't even have grease under his fingernails."

*That's because he was looking at Internet porn all morning and probably already spent his load,* Ida May said after popping up out of nowhere.

"What?" I said, startled by her sudden appearance.

"I said I think he's cheating on me," Moxie said again.

"Right… I mean, you can't know that. Not when you just

have an off feeling." Though wasn't that how most men got caught cheating? When a woman got that little voice inside her head that said something was wrong?

But Moxie shook her head. "No. He's never turned me down before. He's up to something, and I think it's that slutty blonde, Cindy Lou." She took the dustpan from my hand and, without another word, marched into the kitchen.

Julius and I turned to Ida May.

"What are you talking about?" I asked.

She shrugged. *I saw him looking at porn on his phone a couple of hours ago. He was right in there.* She pointed to the living room. *I don't know where the drama queen was, but he was busy taking care of business by himself.*

Julius's mouth popped open. "You spied on him while he was... uh—"

*No.* She gave him an incredulous look. *I left him to it. I didn't want to see his peen. I don't want to see anyone's peen. The gods know I've seen more than my share already.*

"See," I said to Julius. "I told you."

He rolled his eyes.

*Told him what?* Ida May asked, a wicked smile transforming her features. *Were you two discussing my many talents again?*

"Something like that," I said.

"Christ," Julius muttered.

Ida May spun around, twirling her thin nightgown. *If you need pointers, I can help you out.*

"No thanks." Julius, still shaking his head, took off up the stairs. "I think I need a shower."

"Want company?" I called after him just to see his cheeks flush.

Sure enough, when he glanced back at me, his face had turned a pale shade of pink. "Maybe next time."

So much for our afternoon of romance.

*Stick in the mud,* Ida May muttered as she drifted off into the ether once again.

I sighed, and when Moxie's little shih tzu ran into the room, I scooped her up with one hand and started sweeping with the other. The last thing we needed was the rambunctious pup to get glass in her paw.

The puppy wiggled and squirmed, trying to make her escape from my grasp. I glanced down at her. "Don't worry. We'll get this place cleaned up in no time, and you'll once again be free to cause all kinds of mischief."

To my surprise, the dog settled her head against my shoulder and stared up at me with big, golden brown eyes. And dammit if my heart didn't melt right there.

# Chapter 9

"YOU NEVER DID tell me who we're meeting," I said to Julius as he led me up the wooden stairs to the front door of Potions. The brewery was housed in a raised building that sat at the edge of Swamp Lake. The parking lot was filled with a dozen or so custom motorcycles, and the dock had just as many fishing boats moored for the evening. It was the type of place the locals came to and settled in for the night.

Julius didn't answer me as he tightened his grip on my hand and tugged me inside.

"Good evening," the too-thin hostess said, her gaze sweeping over Julius's body. He was wearing trousers, a white button-down shirt, and black suspenders, complete with a fedora. His nineteen twenties fashion sense suited him perfectly, and I couldn't even blame her for staring.

"Hi." Julius smiled at her but pulled me in closer, making it clear we were together. "We're meeting someone. A realtor—"

"Oh, there you are!" The silver-haired fireball we'd met on the bayou tour rushed toward us. She wore bright pink checkered leggings under a black pencil skirt and a matching pink T-shirt that read KISS MY SASS! She topped the look off with scuffed black army boots. She tapped an old weathered mailbag. "I brought a portfolio of listings so we can narrow down what you're looking for. But if you want to see them, you're going to have to find someone with a boat because none of them are accessible by land."

I gaped at Miss Kitty.

"We can do that," Julius said and turned to the hostess. "Three please."

"Miss Kitty already has a table. The skinny blonde waved a hand toward the dining room. "Follow her. I'll have a waitress bring you menus."

"This way." Miss Kitty bounced her way through the restaurant, stopping at a table next to the window wall that overlooked the lake. There was a white card in a metal stand that said: Reserved.

When the hostess had said Miss Kitty already had a table, I hadn't realized she had her own personal table.

"Did you see my video is going viral?" she asked as she slid into the wooden chair. "A producer from *Ghost Hunters* sent me an e-mail already."

"Which video?" I asked, distracted as I spotted Bo across the room, hovering near a heavyset biker. The man wore a gray skullcap and a Twin Forks leather jacket. His beard was no less than a foot long, giving him a grizzly bear look.

"The ghost video from the gator tour this morning. I posted, and it's everywhere. I even saw a bunch of memes posted to Facebook."

"Ida May—Uh, I mean the gator video? You posted it and it went viral?" I asked.

"The gator's name is Buffy," she reminded me, confusing my mention of Ida May for the gator. "And yes. It's everywhere.

I'm expecting a call from News Team Eight any minute now."

"Wow," I said as Julius and I shared an amused glance. "That's... crazy."

"You can say that again." Her phone beeped with an incoming text. "Excuse me," she said. "I have to make a call." The vivacious woman slid out of her chair and retreated back toward the entrance.

"Miss Kitty is the realtor?" I asked Julius, incredulous.

He laughed. "At least she's entertaining."

"It's a wonder she has time to work between her snaps and tweets."

"Her social network of choice is Instagram," he said, opening a menu.

"Whatever. You know she's on all of them. I bet she even has a Tinder account."

"Is that a problem?" Julius asked, raising his eyebrows in challenge.

"No." It was my turn to laugh. "I just don't want to hear her say she has a date to Netflix and chill. I don't want to hear anyone say that. Zombie buttprints were quite enough, thank you."

"Zombie buttprints?" the waitress who'd just arrived at our table asked with a hint of a smile. "Must've been some party."

"I'll say," I muttered and then ordered a beer. Hey, I wasn't the one doing the driving.

After Julius requested a soda and some appetizers, he grabbed Miss Kitty's folder and started going through the available camps for sale.

"This one." I pointed to the flyer that was identical to the one at the real estate office. "It's supposed to be adjacent to the

Twin Forks land."

Julius set it aside along with two others boasting their proximity to the preserve.

I glanced back at the entrance, scanning for Miss Kitty, but she was nowhere to be found. The music had ratcheted up, and the biker crowd had grown by another half dozen men. "I'll be right back," I said as I got up.

"Where are you going?"

"To find us a boat," I said, already heading toward the group of bikers.

The man with the long beard sat at the head of the table and seemed to be holding court as he waved a chicken wing and boasted about a new bike he'd just had delivered that morning. Bo sat behind and to the left of him as if he were a servant waiting for his orders.

I was a few feet away and just about to address the bearded man when he turned to Bo and handed him a bottle of Mudbug ale. "Here, drink this."

I paused. Seriously? He was openly giving a high schooler beer? And no one, not even the waitress, seemed to care as she delivered another round to the entire table.

Bo tipped the beer to his lips and chugged it, not stopping once to take a breath until the bottle was empty.

"Right on, little bro," a tall biker covered in tattoos said as he raised his own beer in a toast.

Bo gave the biker the slightest nod of acknowledgement and then leaned forward to ask Beard something.

Beard scowled and shook his head "Don't push it, boy. Go find out what the hell happened to my gumbo."

"Hey, Bo. When you've managed to find Emerson's gumbo,

grab me a beer?" another biker called, holding his bottle up. "I'm going to be dry soon."

So the guy with the beard was Emerson Charles. I studied him, noting the coldness in his dark eyes as he waited for Bo to heed his order.

After gritting his teeth, the teenager nodded at the other biker, rose, and started to make his way toward the bar where the waitress was waiting for an order to be filled. He wore faded jeans, a solid black T-shirt, and work boots. A chain dangled from his front pocket to one in the back. With the exception of the full-sleeve arm tattoos, he looked like a typical teenager, complete with his sullen expression.

Just before Bo reached the waitress, Emerson called out, "And while you're over there, man up and ask her out. I'm tired of finding nudie magazines in my effing bathroom. Maybe she'll take pity on you and you'll finally get some action."

The crowd roared with laughter while Bo's face first went ghostly white, then quickly turned crimson. He stood there, his head bowed as he balled his hands into fists and every muscle seemed to tense. Then he blew out a long breath, deliberately squared his shoulders, and started moving toward the bar again as if his guardian hadn't just stripped his dignity away in front of practically the entire town.

My chest tightened with anger for the young man. I'd bet my café that wasn't the first time Bo'd been humiliated by Emerson Charles. The bastard. Was the taunting some sort of rite of passage? An initiation into the motorcycle club? Was Bo expected to take whatever they dished out to earn his spot? Or was it worse? Did he have to endure that garbage just to ensure he kept a roof over his head? Either way, no one deserved to suffer such needless humiliation. I bit the side of my cheek to keep from berating the big man right then and there.

A couple of seconds after Bo reached the waitress's side, she turned and called, "Gumbo and beer coming right up, boys!"

She smiled kindly at Bo, slipped her arm around his waist and spoke to him softly. Then she nodded before reaching up to kiss him on the cheek.

Wolf whistles and catcalls erupted from the bikers' table. Bo bent his head to whisper something to the pretty waitress, then retreated back to his group. There were high fives and pats on the back.

"Hit it till she screams your name, little bro," one of the bikers called.

A few others followed up with rutting noises, and one stood and pumped his hips while flicking his tongue at the waitress.

"That's enough," Bo snapped as he shoved the hip thruster, knocking him off-balance. "Say whatever the hell you want to me, but don't disrespect Trina. She's not a piece of meat."

I wanted to pump my fist in the air. Who said chivalry was dead? This kid had heart and plenty of backbone when he was pushed. I hoped that meant he wouldn't put up with their BS for too long.

"The hell she isn't," a lanky ginger said with a snicker.

Bo stopped short and spun around, getting right in the ginger's face. He grabbed him by the shirt and hauled him up out of his chair. "Don't ever—"

A bolt of magic came out of nowhere, hitting Bo directly in the back. He instantly let go of the ginger, seized, then fell to the floor.

Holy hell! I ran to Bo's side, feeling for a pulse. The slow, steady rhythm beat under my fingertips and I looked up, meeting the narrowed eyes of Emerson Charles. "You did this." It wasn't a question. Everyone in the room was staring at him, waiting for him to make another move.

"Who are you?" he asked, his voice full of disdain.

"Someone who's not going to stand by and let a jackass torture this poor kid." Out of the corner of my eye, I spotted Julius hovering nearby. Small sparks of magic glowed in his right hand.

"Did you just call me a jackass?" Emerson asked, his tone more irritated than anything else.

"Yes. There was no reason to attack—"

"Stop," Bo growled and scrambled to his feet. He glanced down at me. "I don't need anyone to defend me."

"But—"

"You heard the boy," Emerson said. "Your *help* isn't welcome here."

I glanced at Bo. "Are you all right? That looked like one heck of a jolt."

"I'm fine," he said, then muttered, "Go. You're making it worse." He then strode back to his seat as if nothing had happened.

Frustrated, I glanced at Julius. His magic had vanished, and he waved for me to join him. My boots hitting the wood floor echoed through the nearly silent restaurant. Apparently I'd helped provide the entertainment for the evening. So much for finding a swamp tour guide. We were halfway back to our table, all eyes still on us.

"Why didn't you do anything?" I asked Julius quietly, so frustrated I was shaking.

"Now?" he asked, glancing down at me. "Bo doesn't need or want that."

"But Emerson attacked him with magic. Can't you call the council or something?"

"I will. After we leave."

It was hard to imagine how Emerson had become the boy's guardian. What social worker in their right mind would place a teen with the gruff, insensitive a-hole? Add in the fact that Emerson was a witch who didn't mind using his powers to discipline, and that meant a recipe for abuse. But I had to admit that Julius had a point; Bo certainly didn't look like he'd appreciate any more of my help. There was nothing to do but head back to the table.

When we were halfway across the room, Emerson called out, "Keep your woman in check, or we'll be forced to do it for you."

I stopped dead in my tracks and spun. "Did you just threaten me?"

*That's the way I heard it,* Ida May said, popping into existence beside me.

I cut my gaze to her for a moment, but I was no longer surprised by her sudden appearances. In fact, they were almost a comfort.

*Want me to kick him in the balls?*

I nearly snorted out a laugh but stopped short when Emerson spoke again. "Got a problem with that, *Ms. Rayne?*"

My humor fled. How did he know my name? No doubt the surprise showed on my face.

*That does it.* Ida May flew over to his table, and even though no one could see her, at least half the bikers at the table turned their heads as if they could feel something was going to happen. And Ida May didn't disappoint. Just as Emerson was about to take a sip of his beer, a knowing smile claimed his lips. But before he could down the amber liquid, Ida May struck out and managed to dislodge his beer from his hand, upending the mug. Liquid flew everywhere—on his face, his shirt, his lap—and then the mug clattered to the floor, managing to somehow not break.

I cleared my throat, holding back my now humorless chuckle. "Don't mess with me, Mr. Charles. You won't like the outcome."

Julius draped an arm over my shoulders. "That's my girl," he said under his breath.

"You did this? What are you, a witch or something?" Emerson sputtered, wiping his face with the back of his hand.

"Not exactly."

He slammed his fist down on the table. "What does 'not exactly' mean?"

I shrugged. "I'm a medium."

"You see the dead?" His eyes narrowed, and he glared as if he didn't believe me. Then he started to rise. "Your kind isn't welcome around here."

"Why's that, Emerson? Too afraid your secrets will come out?" The last words flew out of my mouth before I could stop them. It had been a stupid thing to say, because if he did have something to hide, I'd just borrowed a crap ton of trouble.

"I think it's time we showed you and your boyfriend the door." He started to rise, but before he could lumber out of his chair, Bo put a hand on his shoulder. "Don't bother," he said to the older man. "I'll escort them out."

"Make sure she understands who she's dealing with," Emerson ordered, his lips twisted into a humorless smile.

My ire rose and if I'd had the power, I would've loved to spell him into a gerbil. I suppressed a mocking laugh. The thought of him trapped in cage, running continuously on a wheel, was intensely satisfying. I did have those pre-spelled voodoo dolls back at the inn just waiting curse his junk. Something to look forward to.

Bo strode up to us, his gait a little awkward, and once again I was hit with a powerful burst of déjà vu. He reminded me of someone, but I just couldn't place who. "You'd better go before he loses his patience."

"*Before* he loses it?" I asked, incredulous. "He's a bully."

Bo said nothing, just waved his hand toward the front door.

"But we haven't eaten yet," I said, glancing back at our abandoned table. Miss Kitty still hadn't returned.

"I'll have Trina package it in to-go boxes. It's better if you leave."

"But—"

"Miss Rayne, it's better for all of us if you go."

That shut me up. The last thing I wanted to do was make the situation worse for Bo.

"Come on." Julius grabbed my hand, and together we followed the teenager outside.

"Listen," the teen said, kicking at the gravel. "I'm sorry about him." He glanced up, staring me in the eye, his expression hard and focused. "It's not right the way he treated you."

"It doesn't matter. I'm more concerned about the way he treats you. It's abuse. If you—"

He held his hand up and pressed his lips into a straight line.

"If you think that's abuse, then it's obvious you've never spent time in a foster home."

While I knew his words rang clear with the truth, my heart nearly broke in two for the young boy who was already hardened to the harsh realities of our world. It made me want to wrap him in my arms and then tuck him safely into the spare bedroom back at my apartment.

"Stop looking at me like that," Bo snapped. "I'm not a pity case. Emerson Charles is my guardian. He's an ass, but that's just his way. He thinks he's turning me into a man. It's fine. I'm fine. So just stay out of it, all right?"

"You're sure about that?" Julius asked, eyeing him. "We have resources. Connections to the Witches' Council. I'm sure with a little time we could figure out a better situation for you."

Bo scoffed. "I come from a magical family. No one is going to place me with mundane foster parents. And so far, every witch I've ever met has been crazy. Emerson's no exception. But at least I understand him. No, I'd rather stay put. Only a few more months until graduation, then I'll be free to find my own place."

"Doesn't look like he's going to let you leave the motorcycle club too easily," I said.

"Who said I wanted to leave?" He shoved his hands in his pockets. Then, before I could argue further, he added, "I'll go get your dinner."

Julius handed him a wad of cash. "Tell Trina to keep the change."

Bo nodded and disappeared back inside.

I stared up at Julius, frustrated. First we had virtually no clues about Mia, and now we'd been asked to ignore Emerson

Charles's abusive behavior toward Bo.

"We can't save everyone," Julius said softly, pulling me into his arms.

"I know," I said into his shoulder. "But this one... I don't know if I can let it go. There's something about that kid that makes me want to tuck him under my wing."

"He reminds you of yourself at that age."

I stepped back and glanced up at him. "What do you mean? I still lived with my mom. She was my best friend."

He brought his hand up and gently caressed my cheek. "I know, love. But from what little you've told me, because your mom worked all the time, you were largely on your own with not a lot of financial support. You were taking care of yourself and, I imagine, to some extent your mother too."

The softness in his tone and the understanding yet lack of pity, as if he knew all too well what it meant to have the weight of the world on your shoulders at too young an age, touched me deeply. He'd walked in my shoes, and Bo's, even if his journey had started a century ago. "You're right. I did. And I see how hard it is for him and how much harder it's likely going to get if he doesn't find his way out of that situation."

Julius's hand slipped down my arm until our fingers met and entwined. "The only thing we can do is open doors for him. I'll still contact the council and see what they say. But if he continues to refuse help, you know there's nothing we can do."

I nodded, hating that line of thought. Seventeen-year-old kids learned how to survive. But they often had no idea how to change their circumstances even when opportunities were laid at their feet. The familiar was far more preferable to the unknown.

The door swung open and Bo strode out, carrying a white

paper bag. "Here. She added a piece of cake for the generous tip."

"Thanks, man. Let her know we appreciate it," Julius said, taking the bag.

"Will do."

He turned to leave, but I said, "Hey, Bo. Do you ever do private tours of the bayou?"

He turned around and gave me a skeptical look. "You didn't get enough this morning?"

"Oh sure. Of course. Nothing can beat Buffy the gator and her shenanigans. No. We're looking for a vacation camp, and I was wondering if we could hire you to show us around some of the places only accessible by boat. Like tomorrow maybe? The sooner the better."

He tilted his head as if contemplating my suggestion. Then he said, "A hundred dollars. Cash."

I held out my hand to shake his. "What time?"

He glanced down, then clasped his strong hand over mine. "One p.m. Meet me at the docks."

"We'll be there."

Bo disappeared back into the restaurant, and I glanced around the parking lot once more for Miss Kitty.

"That's her," Julius said, pointing to a monster-style truck. The woman's silver hair was visible against the dark paint.

"Is that hers?" I asked Julius as we crossed the lot.

He laughed. "I really hope so."

When we got closer, I noted the driver's side door was open and Miss Kitty's oversized shoulder bag sat in the front seat. She was busy pacing back and forth, an excited spring in her step.

"I'll be there," she said into the phone. "Anything special

you want me to wear? I hear bright colors are better for TV."

I cleared my throat.

She spun and grinned at us. "Hold on," she said into the phone, then pulled it away from her face as she said, "They're interviewing me tomorrow. I have to be up in New Orleans by nine. Did you find someone with a boat to show you around?"

I nodded. "Tomorrow at one. Bo is taking us. I don't suppose you'll be back by then, will you?" That wasn't a problem for us since we really didn't care about the camps. All we wanted was an excuse to be out on the bayou and hopefully get a glimpse of Bayou Charles.

She shook her head. "No. It's an all-day thing. Then we're coming back here to tape a segment. It's all so exciting. If you want to be part of it, book another morning tour two days from now. They're going to do a reading at the Twin Forks camp."

*Excellent,* Ida May said from behind me. *I know what I'll be doing that morning.*

"But don't worry. All the camps are usually unlocked anyway. No one is stupid enough to go poking around unannounced."

"No one except us," I quipped, giving her an ironic smile.

"Eh, don't worry about. As long as you have Bo with you, no one will bother you. His status with Emerson makes him virtually untouchable." She nodded to the folder still in Julius's hand. "Take a look at whatever you like and let me know if you find a match."

And with that she went back to her phone conversation, asking about a professional makeup artist who knew how to deal with wrinkles.

"Ready to head back to the inn?" Julius asked me.

I nodded, my limbs suddenly exhausted.

*Not me,* Ida May chimed in. *I have a few bikers to harass.* She took off but then called over her shoulder, *Don't do anything I wouldn't do.*

"Shouldn't be a problem," I called back with a wave. Hers was a very short list.

# Chapter 10

I SAT ON the bed, sipping a mocha and nibbling on a chocolate croissant. Not a breakfast of champions, but I was on vacation. And chocolate. Enough said.

Julius walked back into our room, his phone in hand, and frowned. "Not what I wanted to hear."

I raised both eyebrows, waiting. He'd gone outside to contact his superior at the Witches' Council. We were looking for any background information they had on Emerson Charles but wanted to make sure the conversation was private considering that according to Moxie, Hale currently did work for Emerson.

He sighed and sat on the bed next to me. In a hushed tone, he said, "Emerson has restricted status. According to the database, he was caught using a spell to compel someone and is currently on probation. Any use of magic violates his probationary conditions, and now they want me to bring him in."

"You're kidding," I said, putting the croissant down. "Are they sending backup?"

He shook his head. "They want him for questioning only at this time. They said he's been cooperative in the past, so they have no reason to believe he'll resist now."

Crap on toast. Nothing about the biker we'd met the night before said 'cooperative.' I was willing to bet the moment Julius flashed his credentials, Emerson Charles would go into fight-or-flight mode. "We should call Jade."

Jade Calhoun was the New Orleans coven leader, a white witch, and married to my best friend. And while she wasn't involved in any council business, she was the most powerful witch we knew and loyal to a fault. If we called, she'd be here. No questions asked.

"That's a good idea." Julius snagged the discarded bakery bag and pulled out another chocolate-stuffed pastry. "You call. I'm going to eat and finally suck down my coffee." He nodded to his abandoned paper cup sitting on the nightstand, then leaned against the headboard and bit into the croissant. His eyes closed as he savored his breakfast. "If Bettie's Beignets isn't heaven, I don't know what is."

"It's close enough," I agreed and grabbed my mocha on the way out. When I got to the bottom of the stairs, a jingling sound came from behind me, followed by a high-pitched bark. I turned around and grinned. "Well hello there, Miss Stella. How are you today?"

The gold-and-white dog wagged her tail and jumped up on my leg, desperate for attention.

"Good, I see. Come here." I reached down and scooped the little dog up and then peered around for Moxie. She was nowhere to be found. "Looks like it's just you and me, kid," I told the dog. "Wanna come with me?"

Stella responding by licking my face... repeatedly.

I laughed. "Okay, then. Outside we go." Snuggling the

puppy to my chest with one hand and still carrying the mocha with the other, I used my hip to open the screen door that led to the inn's backyard. The space was a maze of pathways lined with greenery and colorful blooms. I followed the path to the right and settled on a wrought iron bench under a cypress tree. Stella curled up in my lap while I called Jade.

"Good morning, sunshine!" Jade said, entirely too chipper. "Why are you up so early?"

I glanced at my watch. "I'd hardly say ten after ten is early." Especially since I was usually up by five every day to open my café.

"It is when you're on vacation with that sexy biker of yours."

I chuckled. "What are you saying? That we're supposed to spend every moment in bed? We're not the ones vying for a medal in the baby-making Olympics." Jade and Kane had recently decided it was time to start a family. And since she was getting some every ten minutes, she'd decided everyone else should too.

"Maybe not, but I sure hope you're taking time to get some practice in, because that's what vacation is for."

"Apparently not this vacation," I said on a sigh.

There was a pause at the other end of the line, then her tone of voice changed and she was all business. "What happened?"

I started at the beginning with our experience with the Swamp Witch, meeting the ghost of Sterling Charles, trying to look for the key, and ended with our run-in with Emerson Charles.

When I was finished, she let out a low whistle. "You two really know how to vacation."

"Stop," I said, smiling into the phone. "We didn't ask for this."

"I know. But it appears Kane and I aren't the only ones who are magnets for trouble."

She had a point. With Jade being a white witch and Kane being a demon hunter, they couldn't seem to go more than a month without some disaster striking. Since Julius had come into my life, we'd ended up in the middle of two murder investigations and I'd been kidnapped twice. Trouble was an understatement. "We learned from the best."

She chuckled. "Touché. All right, let me tie up some loose ends and make sure the café is staffed. Kane and I should be there by tomorrow morning at the latest."

"Thanks," I said, petting the cuddly dog in my lap.

"No thanks necessary. Stay out of trouble long enough for us to at least get into the same zip code."

"No promises," I said, my tone suddenly serious.

She sighed. "I was afraid of that."

After I gave her the details of the inn, we hung up and I sat there on the quiet bench with Stella, enjoying the spring morning. Birds chirped, squirrels scampered up and down the trees, a hummingbird drank his fill at a nearby feeder, and a slight breeze rustled the leaves. It was a completely peaceful moment with nature, something I rarely experienced back on Bourbon Street where I lived and worked. It would have been perfect if it hadn't been for the faint sounds of weeping that came out of nowhere.

I stood, glancing around. There was nothing to see but greenery and red and orange hibiscus blooms.

A muffled sob followed by the snapping of a twig echoed

through the otherwise silent morning.

"Hello?" I called, pressing my hand to my chest.

"Oh God," I heard a woman say on a sob.

Stella lifted her head and stared off to the right on full alert. Her left ear twitched as she sniffed the air, then she took off through the bushes, her high-pitched barks making it easy for me track her.

I jogged down the path and rounded the corner just in time to see Moxie dart back into the house and slam the door on Stella. The little dog growled and scratched at the door, clearly upset to be left outside.

What the heck? "Here, girl," I said and squatted to once again pick up the dog. I lifted her into the crook of my arm and asked, "What was that about, do you think?"

Stella glanced from me to the door and back again.

"Yeah, that's what I thought too." Moxie had run from me. But why? Had she overheard my conversation with Jade? If so, why would she be crying? She'd have just learned her friend might still be alive.

Taking a deep breath, I opened the door and strode into the house. It wasn't hard to figure out where she'd gone. There were dirty footprints leading from the back door, through the living room, and disappearing behind the closed door of Hale's office. I knocked once.

"Yes?" Moxie said, her voice surprisingly clear.

"It's Pyper. I just wanted to make sure you were okay."

"I'm fine," she said her, voice rising on the word *fine* as if she was trying to keep herself from crying.

"Come on, Moxie, you don't really seem fine. Would you open the door please?"

The door swung open and Moxie stood there, her jeans splattered with dirt and a sunflower in her hand. Her eyes were red and puffy, but her cheeks were dry. Stella lifted her head from my chest and barked once at her owner.

"Stop barking at me, Stella," Moxie said, sounding exasperated. Then she tilted her head, studying me. "How did you do that?"

"Do what?" I asked as Stella pressed her little face into my shoulder.

"Pick her up. It took me a week before she'd let me touch her after the rescue dropped her off. Most persnickety foster dog ever."

"She's been letting me pick her up ever since she busted into our room," I said and added, "You're fostering her? I thought she was yours."

She shook her head. "Nope. She needs a house with no other dogs apparently. I took her in three months ago, and still no one wants her. Or I should say she doesn't want them. But you… Looks like she just adopted you."

"What?" I lifted the dog away from me, holding her out at arm's length. She just looked at me and yawned. "I can't have a puppy. I work. I…" But my protests were hollow to my own ears as I pulled her back in, enjoying the warmth of her body against my chest. Of course I could have a dog. I lived upstairs from my coffee shop. Running up to take care of her wasn't an issue. And it wasn't like Kane, the owner of the building, was going to say no.

"I don't think you have a choice," Moxie said as Stella reached out one paw and pressed it to my face.

My heart melted right there, and I knew I was a goner. I

smiled at Moxie. "I think you're right."

"I'll let the rescue know. I'm sure they'll have some paperwork for you." She gave me a sad smile and started to close the door.

"Wait!" I held up a hand. "I came to find you because you seem upset. Is there anything I can do besides take Stella off your hands?"

She didn't say anything for a minute, then blurted, "Yeah. Next time you see that two-timing bastard Hale, kick him in the balls and tell him I'm tired of his crap. I did anything that man asked me to, and this is how he repays me. Well, eff that. If he wants someone to play Buffy to his Spike, he can just ask Emerson Charles to dress up like a slayer. I'm done!"

The door slammed so hard Stella nearly jumped right out of my arms.

"Whoa, girl," I said soothingly, calming her down.

"Buffy to his Spike?" Julius asked from behind me. "Who are Buffy and Spike?"

I turned and couldn't help the amused smile playing on my lips. "Only the best TV couple of all time. Clearly we need to carve out some time to get you caught up on pop culture."

"The best? Didn't you just say the same thing about Damon and Elena last week?"

I snorted. *The Vampire Dairies* was one of my guilty pleasures, and I didn't hesitate to make Julius watch it with me. "I can't believe you were paying attention."

His eyes softened, and everything inside me turned to mush. "I'm always paying attention."

My heart swelled and I leaned in to kiss him softly.

His arms went around me, and if it hadn't been for the

squirming puppy between us, I was fairly certain we'd have ended up in a make-out session right there in the inn's living room. Instead, he gave me a slow, lingering kiss, then let me go as he eyed Stella. "Don't be getting ideas, little girl. You already goosed me once."

Laughter bubbled up as I held Stella out to him. "Get used to her, Julius. It appears we have a new roommate. When we leave, she's coming home with us."

"When did this happen?"

I explained her foster-care status and then shrugged. "It appears she's adopted me."

He stared at both of us for a moment, then shrugged. "Can't blame her. After all, I was a stray who just showed up too." He winked, took Stella from me, and stared her in the eye. "Just one stipulation, you hear? No more ass biting. It's not cool."

# Chapter 11

"J ADE'S GOING TO have to take Stella home with her," I said as I climbed off the back of Julius's bike. "A dog can't ride on this thing."

"Why not?" Julius grabbed my hand and led me down to the docks. We were back at Mayhem Gator Tours to meet with Bo for our private ride through the bayou. "You can just get one of those doggie backpacks. I bet she'd love it."

"You're kidding right?" I tried to picture Stella strapped to my back and immediately shook my head. "It's not safe."

"We can get her doggie goggles." Julius grinned.

"And a helmet? Nope." I shook my head. "As adorable as that sounds, I'm not letting my baby on the back of a bike." *My baby?* Jeez. I'd known the pup for two, three days, had just decided to welcome her into my home, and I was already acting the overbearing doggie mama. Poor thing. She was going to be smothered.

"You sound like you're talking about your teenage daughter," Julius said.

I shrugged. "Her too. If I had one." I grinned at him. "You bikers are trouble."

"When it comes to scoring with the hot chicks, it pays to be the bad boy." He slipped his arm around me and pulled me close until our bodies melded together. Then he bent his head and nipped playfully at my lower lip. "The bike is just an added bonus."

I smiled up at him, ready to lift my lips to his, but stopped short when we heard the squeal of tires in the gravel parking lot.

"Get in the car. Now!" an unfamiliar voice shouted.

Julius and I both took off down the path with me a few feet in front of him. More unintelligible shouting filled the air, and when I rounded the corner of the building, I spotted Bo towering over a stocky man who wore a Twin Forks motorcycle jacket. Both were red faced and yelling over each other. A mud-splattered black SUV sat idling a few feet away. The stocky guy swung, but Bo jumped back, easily avoiding the blow.

"Hey!" I cried out. "Leave the kid alone!"

Bo twisted, meeting my eyes. "Back off, Pyper."

But when he did, Stocky grabbed his arm, twisted it behind his back, and then shoved Bo in the vehicle. The car was already rolling when Stocky climbed in after him. Stocky leaned out the window and said, "Better find yourself a new guide; looks like Keybo has other plans today."

The tires spun and gravel sprayed across the lot as the SUV roared out of the parking lot.

I turned to Julius with my mouth open. "Did you hear that?"

Julius nodded. "Sounds like Bo's given name is Keybo."

"Son of a… We were never looking for a key. We were looking for Bo." I grabbed Julius's arm, clinging to him desperately. "We need to follow that SUV. Now."

"Let's go." Julius shook my hold loose, but instead of

running to the bike, he sprinted over to where Bo and Stocky had been arguing and bent to retrieve something.

A ball cap.

I recognized it as one Bo had been wearing the day before. I let out a small sigh of relief. With something that belonged to Bo, Julius could cast a finding spell. Though without the help of the coven or a circle, it would be a weak one at best.

"Pyper!" Julius called, already standing by the bike.

I mentally cursed myself and ran over to him. Standing around wasn't going to do us any favors if we wanted to help Bo.

"Hold this," Julius said, handing me the camouflage-print ball cap.

I took it, holding it by the bill, waiting for Julius to do his thing.

He held out a hand, a pale sheen of light covering his fingertips. Then he closed his eyes, touched the top of the hat, and said, "Woven threads, make the connection, be the link to whom we seek." The magic brightened and then shot from each fingertip in a sudden burst of energy, skittering over the hat until the entire thing was covered in magical light. The bill heated between my fingertips as if the thing would suddenly burst into flames.

Then I felt the zap of a small shock just before the magic winked out, leaving only one small dot of light hovering in the air between us.

"Come on." Julius climbed on the bike, already adjusting his helmet as I jumped onto the seat behind him. Seconds later, Julius said, "Find Keybo."

The light glowed brighter and shot ahead, turning right, the same way the SUV had gone. We shot down the two-lane highway, following the orb. It zigzagged in front of us as if continually searching for the correct path and suddenly took a left turn just as we were rolling through an intersection. Julius hit the brakes, causing the bike to skid slightly. He righted the beast and followed the orb.

The trees and vegetation were thick overhead, blocking out the afternoon sun. Driveways and dirt roads were blocked off with weatherworn gates and signs that said: No Trespassing, Keep Out, and Beware of Alligators.

Another turn followed by at least a half dozen more eventually led us down a dirt road. Dust billowed in a cloud behind us as the orb slowed and eventually stopped at a dead end. Julius cut the motor, and we glanced around at the unruly vines overtaking the trees. There weren't any new roads or driveways.

We both climbed off the bike.

I studied the tire tracks in the dirt. "It looks like someone has been down here recently."

"They didn't stay long," Julius said, indicating the tracks that formed a U-turn. He turned to the still hovering orb. "Find Keybo."

The orb rose in the air, moved in a wide circle, reversed course, and then flew directly at me, hitting me squarely in the chest. A small jolt of static electricity shot through me, making me catch my breath as I stumbled back.

"Whoa." I rubbed at my chest, more out of surprise than any sort of physical pain. "What the heck happened there?"

Julius frowned. "That was… not supposed to happen."

"Obviously." I let out a sigh. "Sometimes I hate magic."

That got a tiny smile out of him. "Would you rather it didn't exist?"

I stared at him, meeting his dark eyes, and shook my head. Without magic, Julius wouldn't be in my life. And that thought was unacceptable.

His smile widened a touch and he pulled me to him, wrapping his strong arms around me. "Are you all right?"

I pressed my head to his chest and nodded. "Yes. Just worried. I don't like whatever mess Bo is caught up in. And now that I know Sterling Charles most likely sent us to look for him, I don't know what to make of anything. Why would Sterling send us to Bo? Surely if he knew anything about Mia's disappearance, he'd have said something about it, right?"

"Not necessarily. It's possible he has information he shouldn't and is too afraid to say anything."

"I guess so," I said as foreboding took up residence in my gut. The idea that Bo knew anything about Mia's disappearance was gut-wrenching. That meant when she disappeared, he couldn't have been any older than twelve or thirteen. Something like that could screw a kid up for the rest of his life. "If someone in the motorcycle club is responsible for Mia's disappearance, they might all be covering and coercing Bo to do the same. Or if Emerson has anything to do with her disappearance, that would be a huge problem for Bo as well."

We were silent for a long moment, then I pulled back. "We're not going to solve anything by just standing here."

"No. We're not." Julius pressed his lips together in a thin line and rubbed at the scruff on his jawline. Then he peered at me. "You should not have been able to absorb that orb."

"It's not like I was trying." I placed my hands on my hips

and tapped my foot. "Now we have no way to find Bo."

"I know you weren't. I'm just concerned that the spell attached itself to you. That's not normal."

I pulled Bo's cap out of my back pocket. "Maybe it's because I still have this."

"Maybe," he said but didn't sound convinced. "That would be pretty unusual." He took the ball cap from me, studied it, and then tucked it into one of the saddlebags on the bike. "When Jade gets here, we'll use this to try another finding spell. Until then, I think it's best we head on back to town."

Clouds had formed out of nowhere, and the bayou suddenly became dark with shadows. A chill ran up my spine, and it had nothing to do with the temperature. "Yeah. Let's get out of here."

We took off back down the dirt road and made a left, then a right, then a left, but when we came to a four-way stop, Julius planted his feet and turned to look at me. "Does this look familiar?"

I shook my head. Trees lined one side of the road while open water lapped at the other. "I don't remember that body of water."

"Me neither. Dammit." Julius turned around on the deserted road, and after two more turns he stopped again, this time in front of a gated driveway. "We're going to need to map our way out of here."

I nodded and pulled my phone out but then grimaced. "No service."

Julius dug around until he found his phone, then shook his head. "Same."

"Just drive until we find a gas station or store or something.

We'll find our way out eventually," I said, hearing the echo of Otis's voice in my mind. *Don't ever head into unknown territory out there. You're likely to run into the live end of a shotgun.*

Well, there was nothing else we could do. Staying on the side of the road wasn't an option.

Julius shoved his phone into his pocket, fired up the motorcycle once more, and took off down the road. Everything looked the same, familiar but not. Greenery and cypress trees and water was everywhere. Had we been down this road before? I couldn't be certain. The skies were darkening with thunderclouds, and shadows cast us in darkness.

Then the first of the fat raindrops started to fall.

Son of a monkey. I gritted my teeth and pressed my face to Julius's back. There was nothing worse than riding on a motorcycle during a rainstorm.

Soaked to the bone, Julius finally pulled over, seeking shelter under the overhang of a deserted gas station. We climbed off and huddled together while we waited for the worst of the storm to blow through. We'd been standing there for a good twenty minutes when we spotted headlights on the road.

"I'm going to wave them down," I told Julius right before I shot off to the side of the road. The rain started to let up, and I sighed in relief. If we had any idea which way to go, we could get back on the road and hopefully make it out of there before the sun set completely.

I waved my hands and shouted, "Stop!"

The white truck slowed.

"Stop!" I cried again, jumping up and down.

The truck pulled into the defunct gas station. I ran over as the man rolled the window down.

"That bike givin' yous trouble?" he asked, peering through the still falling rain.

"No we're—Otis?" I asked in surprise as I recognized the grizzled face I'd seen every day since we'd wandered into Mayhem. "What are you doing out here? I thought you were married to that restaurant."

He blinked, then recognition flashed over his weathered face. "It's you."

I smiled, holding my hands over my head as if that would shield me from the rain. "It's me."

"Didn't I tell ya not to go skulking around the bayou?" He scowled and reached up to tap the shotgun mounted behind his head. "You're askin' for trouble, little girl. Go back to town before someone decides to feed you both to the gators."

Surly old man. "We're trying, but we took a wrong turn and can't seem to find the main highway. Do you think you can point us in the right direction? If you've got a minute that is," I said, raising my eyebrows as I spied a bouquet of red roses on his passenger seat. There were also a couple of cartons of takeout next to them and what appeared to be a pie box. "Looks like you've got a date."

He put his hand over the flowers as if that would hide them and shook his head. "It's nothing. Tell that young man of yours to follow me. I'll lead you out of here."

"You got it. Thanks, Otis. You're the best. And tell your date we appreciate it too."

"I don't have a date," he grumbled and then yanked the steering wheel and made a U-turn.

I chuckled as I ran back to Julius and told him to hurry up. The sooner we got back to the inn and into dry clothes, the better.

# Chapter 12

THE HOT WATER sluiced over me, warming my chilled bones as I stood in the shower. We'd finally made it back to the inn, relieved that Stella was the only one to greet us. Neither Moxie nor Hale were anywhere to be found. Thank the gods, because I was too busy worrying about Bo and Mia to deal with another Moxie meltdown.

The image of the biker shoving Bo into the SUV kept playing over and over in my mind. What were they making him do? Where had they taken him? Every part of my being was screaming a warning that the Twin Forks motorcycle gang was Trouble with a capital *T*. And they were seriously messing up that poor kid. As for Mia, I'd bet my last dollar Emerson Charles had her stashed somewhere. Likely Sterling had sent us to Bo because there was no hope of getting anyone else in the club to talk.

"Pyper!"

I poked my head around the shower curtain and found Julius frowning as he stood in the doorway holding Stella. "Yes?"

"Your dog is losing her mind."

I glanced at the pup cuddled against his chest. "You sure

about that?"

He gave me a flat stare. "Just finish up, will you? She's been barking at the door since you got in there."

I laughed. "Seriously?"

"Seriously." He gently put Stella on the floor and then shut her in the bathroom with me.

"Are you going to behave?" I asked her.

She let out a yelp and ran past the curtain into the shower, circled around my feet, and darted back out.

"I guess not." I turned the water off, and after I was once again dressed in clean clothes, I dried Stella off and carried her back into the room.

Julius sat on the bed, computer open as he pecked around on the keyboard with both index fingers.

"If you're going to continue to try to type up your notes, you might want to take a typing class," I said, smiling.

"I'm fine." He closed the computer and stared at Stella. "That dog is already spoiled rotten."

I glanced down at her and patted her still-wet head. "I have no idea what you're talking about."

"Right." Julius climbed off the bed, paused to kiss my temple, and then disappeared into the bathroom for his own shower.

I put the little troublemaker on the floor, picked up my phone, and typed in Twin Forks Cycles. Since we'd lost Bo, Emerson Charles's garage was the most obvious place to check out next.

I'd just landed on the bed when Stella's piercing bark filled the room. I glanced down, spotting her standing in front of the rocking chair, her teeth bared.

"Hush, Stella," I commanded and went back to studying the route to Twin Forks. The last thing we needed was to get lost in the bayou again.

Stella went on another barking jag, this time accompanied with a snarl.

I got up and reached for her, but just as I was about to pick her up, she lunged forward and latched onto... nothing.

"Ouch! You little schnitzel. Get off!" Ida May suddenly appeared in front of the rocking chair and kicked her leg out, dislodging Stella from her ankle. Ida May turned to me, hands on her hips. "You can't take that thing home."

I glanced back and forth between the two.

Stella cowered next to my feet, shaking slightly while Ida May scowled at both of us. "Did you see what she just did? She nearly took a toe off."

I reached out a hand, waving it right through Ida May's transparent body.

"Hey!" She jerked away and proceeded to float back and forth as if she was pacing in midair. "That was rude. Wait until you're a ghost and someone violates your space." She shivered and wrapped her arms around herself. "Not cool."

"Sorry," I said, rubbing my forehead. "I'm just trying to figure out how a dog bit a ghost. I mean, I know you've been solid a time or two before, but... you're clearly not now."

Ida May stopped and stared at the dog. "How *did* you do that?"

Stella barked once, ran forward, and wiggled her little body in excitement. It appeared that since she could now see and hear Ida May, she was no longer afraid of the ghost.

"Oh, cut it out." Ida May reached down and picked Stella

up with both hands, holding the little dog out in front of her. A huge grin spread over the ghost's face as Stella started to wag her tail.

I widened my eyes in surprise. "This is not normal."

Tears filled Ida May's eyes as she pulled the little puppy in close and snuggled her. "Nothing is normal around you," Ida May said, smiling. She closed her eyes and rocked back and forth in pure bliss.

I just stood there, my heart swelling at Ida May's sudden happiness. What must it be like to be a ghost and then suddenly be able to connect with another living being?

"I'm going to call her Twinkles and feed her pigs in a blanket." Ida May grinned at me.

"Twinkles? Her name is Stella," I said, amused at Ida May's abrupt change of heart.

"She tried to take a toe off. It seems fitting." Then Ida May sat down in the rocker and Stella, aka Twinkles, curled up in her lap, blissed out as Ida May scratched behind her ears.

✧   ✧   ✧

"I'm telling you," I said to Julius as we peered into the darkened windows of the small green building marked Twin Forks Cycles. The door was locked and no one had answered when we knocked. "I've never seen anything like it. Stella can interact with Ida May as if she's a solid, in-the-flesh, human being. The dog nipped her foot for goodness' sake. How is that possible?"

Julius shook his head. "I have no idea. Never encountered something like that in all my years. Maybe Stella has an affinity for ghosts, and that's why she bonded with you but not Moxie."

I shrugged. "Maybe. But it looks like Ida May has a new best friend. Of course we'll be expected to feed her, take her to the vet, and get her groomed. "But there's no doubt in my mind that Stella is going to have Ida May wrapped around her little finger."

Julius shook his head again, only this time in mild disbelief. "A dog that bonds with Ida May. Now I've seen everything."

"Maybe not quite everything." I pointed down the gravel driveway toward the open garage that sat behind the main building.

"Christ," Julius muttered. Inside we spotted Hale stripping his jeans and black T-shirt off, leaving him only in hot-pink boy shorts. "I don't think society is moving in the right direction if that is an acceptable fashion choice."

I snickered. "Is it the shiny material or the color that's the most offensive to you?"

"Both. And the fact that they are so tight they leave nothing to the imagination. I do not need that image plastered in my brain."

He had a point. Hale's junk was on full display. "Just avert your eyes."

"Hard to do when a two-hundred-pound man is strutting around like a Playmate."

I raised my eyebrows in question. "Playmate, huh? Since when do you read *Playboy*?"

"I don't. Err, not anymore. But it was damned boring being a ghost sometimes. Pretty much any form of entertainment would do."

"Right." I let the subject drop as I watched Hale climb into overalls. After shoving his feet back into his work boots, he picked up a wrench and went to work on one of the many Harleys occupying the shop. The sharp stench of motor oil filled my senses as we entered the bay. And because the music was blaring, he didn't notice us until we were only a few feet away.

His head suddenly jerked up when our shadows fell across the bike. He pulled out a remote and muted the radio as a dark shade of red stained his cheeks. "Julius... Pyper. Uh, when did you two get here?"

"Just now," I said, staring past his shoulder in an effort to not snicker as the image of him in hot-pink undies flashed through my mind. "We parked in front of the shop. You probably didn't hear our bike because of the music."

He glanced down the lane toward the office. "The customer service department isn't actually open right now. Did you need something? I could take a look at your bike if—"

"No. The bike is fine," Julius said. "We're actually here looking for Bo."

"Bo?" Hale frowned. "He doesn't usually work in the shop."

"Yeah, I know," I said. "But we had an appointment with him this afternoon for a private swamp tour, and when we got Mayhem Tours, a couple of the guys from the Twin Forks Motorcycle Club forced him into their SUV. To be honest, I'd like to make sure he's okay."

Hale rubbed his left shoulder and averted his gaze. "Ah, that's nothing to worry about. I'm sure the boys are just messing around. I'll get him the message to call you."

Julius and I shared a glance. Hale couldn't even look us in the eye.

I cleared my throat. "Where do you think your boys would

take him?"

Hale's brow pinched as his dark eyes finally met mine. "I don't think this is something you should be worried about." He glanced at the clock and sucked in a short breath. "In fact, I think it's best if y'all go now. Emerson doesn't really like people hanging around the shop. It's a liability thing."

"Listen," I said, trying my best to rein in my frustration. "I'm really uncomfortable with what I saw earlier. I'd feel a lot better if I could just talk to Bo. So if you could help us out here with any suggestions on where to find him, I'd really appreciate it."

Hale pressed his lips together, opened his mouth, then shut it and shook his head. "I don't know what to tell you. I'm sure he'll be at work in the morning."

*He knows*, a male voice said from behind me.

I glanced over my shoulder and spotted the biker Sterling Charles floating toward us.

*He's just too afraid of Emerson to say anything.*

"Why?" I asked the ghost.

"What do you mean, why?" Hale asked, frowning at me. "If he wants to get paid, he'll be there."

I ignored Hale and gave Sterling my full attention.

The biker studied Hale and then curled his right hand into a fist as if he was dying to take a swing at the man. And who could blame him? Hale's lack of concern for the teenager made me want to kick him in the junk. *Because Emerson has dirt on everyone who works for him. It's how he motivates them to do whatever he asks. I don't know what he has on Hale, but you can bet it's something dirty. Tell him Mia's alive and that Bo is the key to finding her. That will get him talking.*

"Bo *is* the key, then?" I blurted out, but before Sterling could answer, he vanished into thin air. "Dammit!" I kicked a stray screwdriver, sending it skirting across the cement floor. "Why does he keep disappearing on me?"

"You know the answer to that," Julius said, his tone calm. "It used to happen to me all the time."

He was right, of course. When I'd first met Julius in his ghost form, he'd appear and then disappear when he'd exhausted his store of energy. It was likely the same for Sterling. Talk about frustrating. There was nothing like getting vague, cryptic messages about a five-year-old abduction case.

"What are you two talking about?" Hale asked, confusion lining his face. "Bo is the key to what? And why do you two care so much about that kid?"

"Tell him," Julius said.

I turned and looked Hale straight in the eye. "We have reason to believe that Mia is still alive and that Bo can lead us to her."

# Chapter 13

HALE TOOK A step back, bumping into a rolling toolbox. The red chest moved a few inches and knocked into the bike he'd been working on, causing the entire thing to crash to the ground. The echo of metal on concrete filled the garage, but Hale didn't even seem to notice. "What did you just say?"

"We have reason to believe Mia is still alive. Bo seems to be the key to finding her," I said again.

Hale shook his head. "No. I don't know what people have been telling you, but you've got entirely the wrong idea. Bo would never hurt his sister. Not for anybody or any reason."

"Bo is Mia's brother?" I gasped out. Holy hell balls. Was he serious? Did that mean Bo was living with the man who was responsible for Mia's disappearance? My stomach rolled, and I felt bile rise up in the back of my throat.

"You didn't know that?" Hale started pacing the garage and grimaced when he noticed the fallen motorcycle. "Where did you get that information? Because whoever that jackass is, he or she is stirring up trouble you don't need. If I were you, I'd climb right back on that bike of yours and leave this town before someone decides you're more trouble than you're worth."

"Is that a threat?" Julius asked, taking a half step in front of me.

"No. It's a fact." Hale glanced up at the big wall clock, grimaced again, and then pointed down the drive. "It's time for you to go."

"No," I said quietly. "Not until you tell us where we can find Bo. He and Mia are both in trouble, and I'm not leaving until you help us."

"You don't—"

"Listen, Hale." I moved forward until I was right in front of him. "There are things about me I should probably explain."

The man pulled a greasy rag out of his pocket and gripped it with both hands. "I don't care if you're the governor of Louisiana or a voodoo priestess with the power to curse my manhood," he said between clenched teeth. "If you don't get out of here in the next few minutes, there's going to be hell to pay."

I laughed. "I'm neither the governor nor a voodoo priestess, but I am a medium, and guess who was just here?"

"A medium? As in a ghost whisperer?" He let out a mocking laugh of his own. "Stop playing games, Pyper. Now isn't the time." He grabbed my upper arm and started to pull me out of the garage.

"Hale, let go of her," Julius said, a low growl in his voice. "Now."

"I'm just escorting her off the property," Hale said without looking back.

A crackle sounded from behind us, and Hale froze. He turned and glanced over his shoulder. His eyes widened, fear rolling through them as he let me go.

I rubbed my bicep and eyed Julius. Magical light shimmered

over his right hand and halfway up his arm. "It's okay," I said, trying to defuse the situation.

"It's not."

"Dude." Hale held both hands up. "There's no need for any of that magic stuff. I'm just trying to protect you both."

"And we're trying to save Mia and Bo." I let out an exaggerated sigh. "Listen. Sterling told me Mia is still alive and that Bo is the key to finding her. That doesn't mean Bo has anything to do with her disappearance, but he most certainly has some information that can help us find her. And on top of that, if Emerson has anything to do with her disappearance, then that means Bo could be in trouble too. So please, Hale. If you have any idea where Bo is, tell me now. If not for them then for Moxie. You know how much she misses her friend."

Hale's face went ghost-white at the mention of Moxie. Then his shoulders slumped and he gave me a small nod. "I might know something. But you have to promise to be careful. Emerson is—"

"Right behind you." Emerson's deep voice preceded him as he slipped out of the shadows of the garage.

"Emerson… uh, when did you… um, I didn't know you were here," Hale stammered as he moved to give the man a wide berth.

Emerson scowled at his employee and raised his hand, fingers curled as if he were gripping something.

Hale's eyes bulged and he gasped as his air was cut off while he clawed at the invisible vise clasped around his throat.

"Clearly you haven't learned your lesson from the last incident." Emerson inched closer, his expression stone-cold. "What's it going to take to make sure you keep that big trap shut?" Emerson reached into his pocket and pulled out a folded Buck knife. Without so much as a flick of his hand, the knife popped open while Emerson moved toward Hale. "Maybe we need to do something about that tongue of yours."

"Emerson!" I cried, my heart pounding against my rib cage. "What the hell—"

"*Duratus!*" Julius's entire body shook in rage as he poured magic into Emerson.

The large biker seized in place, and the knife fell harmlessly to the floor, skittering under one of the large rolling tool boxes.

Hale collapsed in a heap, gasping in air.

I ran to his side, helping him sit up. "Are you okay?"

His mouth worked, but no sound came out. Then he shook his head, his eyes watering.

*Emerson spelled him into silence. It'll probably last a few days.* Sterling once again floated near me. *It's one of his talents.*

"Do you know where Bo is?" I asked the ghost.

*No. But when you find him, he will eventually lead you to Mia.*

Emerson shook Julius's spell off and immediately unleashed two streams of dark green magic. The first one hit Julius right in the chest, sending him crashing into the wall of the garage while the other encapsulated Sterling in a giant green web. Emerson turned to his brother and roared, "I told you not to come back here again!"

Sterling's face contorted in anger, but then the magic pulsed around his form and the ghost disintegrated right before our eyes.

I clasped my hand over my mouth and gasped, my eyes immediately locking on Julius's. I swallowed to dislodge my heart, which had gotten caught in my throat at the sight of him. He was disheveled and appeared a little dazed, but he was whole and largely undamaged as far as I could tell.

Emerson moved to stand next to me and glared down at Hale. "Stop your whimpering and get back to work. Smithy will be here within the hour."

Hale nodded once, picked up his wrench with a shaky hand, and stumbled over to the abandoned Harley.

I stood, rage coursing through my veins. Stalking toward him, I said, "Who do you think you are, throwing your magic around like that?"

Magic skittered across his skin as he turned his wild eyes on me. "You don't want a piece of this, little girl."

"Little girl?" I scoffed and jabbed my finger into his chest. "You're a damned bully. And I, for one, am not going to let you get away with it." My anger had taken over and forced out any shred of fear. This man had silenced Hale, banished his brother's ghost, and worst of all, attacked my boyfriend. Clearly he didn't know who he was dealing with. No one messed with those I cared about.

Emerson looked me up and down, glanced past me over my shoulder, and then laughed meanly. "Doesn't look like your knight in shining armor is up to saving your sweet ass, so maybe it's best you just give him a hand dragging himself off my land before I shoot you for being on private property."

I glanced back at Julius and fought the urge to run to his side. He'd gotten himself up on both feet, but he was leaning over a stainless steel table while balancing on one foot. His face was contorted in pain as he used one hand to clutch his knee.

"You soulless bastard," I said to Emerson, my tone low and

SPIRITS, BEIGNETS, AND A BAYOU BIKER GANG

full of hatred. "What is wrong with you?"

Emerson Charles turned his head slowly until he was staring me dead in the eye. The mean arrogance he'd possessed since he'd walked into the garage had disappeared and was replaced by an eerie coldness that sent a chill straight to my heart. "Don't ever imply there's anything wrong with me."

"Hit a sore spot, did I?" I shot back. "Well, too freakin' bad. Because from where I'm standing, you have some serious issues, buddy. But honestly, I don't even care. All I want is for you to reverse that silencing spell you put on Hale and to tell me where Bo is. Then we'll just get out of your way." And even though I knew the council had told Julius to bring Emerson in for questioning, I meant what I'd said. I didn't give two figs about the seething man in front of me. All I wanted was to get Julius out of there as soon as possible, make sure Bo was okay, and find Mia. I couldn't care less about whatever else was going on.

"Bo is busy doing a job for me," Emerson said, his expression still void of any emotion. "And Hale is my employee. If he doesn't like the way he's treated, he can quit at any time."

Hale let out a disgruntled huff and shook his head, but he didn't look at either one of us. Clearly the man was only there out of some sort of debt or obligation to Emerson Charles.

"If you've got a problem with our arrangement, you know where the door is, Allman."

Hale met the biker's gaze, then lifted his hand and flipped him off.

Emerson stood up straight, seemingly growing a few inches taller as his neck and face flamed red. All the muscles in his arms and shoulders flexed just before he lunged for Hale, his hands ablaze with fire.

Hale's eyes widened and his mouth opened in a silent scream as he jumped back, trying and failing to stay out of Emerson's reach.

"No!" I cried as I rushed forward, my hand automatically reaching for the knife Avrilla had given me.

Then all hell broke loose.

Hale brought one leg up, kicking out against Emerson's attack, but the biker managed to get hold of Hale's foot at exactly the same time ice-blue magic exploded from Julius, coating Emerson. The fire consuming his hands vanished, leaving only black smoke in its place. But it was too late. Just below the knee, Hale's overalls had caught fire.

Hale panicked and ran toward the open garage door but slipped and fell. He immediately started rolling around, trying to snuff the fire out. But because of the grease staining the fabric, the action was fruitless. I glanced around, frantically looking for a fire extinguisher. Nothing. I couldn't see one near any door or any other obvious place a garage should have one.

My head started to pound, and behind me, I heard the crackle of magic, followed by grunts and shouts of frustration. Emerson and Julius were in a serious magical duel, but I couldn't worry about that. My one and only concern was Hale. We had to get him out of those overalls.

I sprinted to his side. "Hold still," I ordered.

The fear in his eyes resembled that of a wild animal. I placed my hand on his chest, gently holding him down and said, "Trust me. You're going to be okay."

He sucked in a deep breath and stilled. I gripped the knife still in my other hand and immediately sliced through the denim shoulder straps of his overalls,

"Get up!" I yanked on his arm, pulling him to his feet despite the flames licking their way up to his thighs.

Then without another word, I yanked the overalls down, ignoring the heat singeing my hands.

Hale finally sprang into action, frantically kicking his shoes off as he jumped out of the still-flaming denim. Wiping his brow, he stood beside me as we both watched the overalls go up in flames.

"Are you all right?" I asked, ignoring his hot-pink boy shorts.

He nodded hastily, taking deep breaths as if to calm himself down. Satisfied he wasn't in any immediate danger, I turned my attention to the magical showdown still happening across the garage.

Son of a...! Emerson Charles had retreated and was muttering to himself while Julius worked on freeing himself from an intricate green net as if he'd gotten caught in Emerson's magical web. Each time Julius zapped a portion of the net, making it disappear, the net started to grow back. It was so fast Julius was barely making any progress.

Emerson shot a stream of magic toward a heavy spool of stainless steel chain. The spool started to turn and the chain unraveled, working its way into a spiral around Julius.

"Oh my god! Have you lost your ever-loving mind?" I yelled, already running across the garage with the knife still clutched in my hand. I didn't have magic, or at least not any I could access without a little bit of help, and the knife was literally my only hope of helping Julius out of his bind.

There was no hesitation. And the guttural groan that came from Julius as Emerson Charles tightened the chains only spurred me on. Without any thought for my own safety, I lunged forward, barely dodging a bolt of magic Emerson flung my way, and brought the knife down only inches from his fingertips. I'd been aiming to cut off the magical stream manipulating the chain that was now squeezing Julius like a steel boa constrictor.

The knife bounced off the concrete-like magic, sending a jolt that shot straight to my shoulder and causing me to drop the knife. I fell to one knee, holding my arm and gasping air to breathe through the pain.

"You're an annoying pain in the ass," Emerson said, disgust in his tone.

"I'm the annoying pain in the ass that is going to kick you in the balls," I said, reaching for my knife as I got to my feet. "And then cut them off if you don't release Julius." I was done messing around with this good-for-nothing lowlife.

"What did you say?" he snarled, his eyes going black with anger.

"You heard me." I brandished the knife. "What's the matter? Too much of a coward to tangle with a 'little girl'?"

"You're going to regret you ever laid eyes on me." Emerson dropped the steady stream of magic he'd been pumping into Julius. A second later, I heard the clank of metal against the concrete floor, followed by a grunt as my boyfriend fell to the floor. But there was no time to check on him. Right then I had my hands full. Because that fire Emerson Charles had conjured earlier was back, and he was already reaching for me.

"No!" I jumped to the side, and this time instead of aiming for his magic, I went for his shoulder. What was it Avrilla had said?

*All this requires is a drop of blood to keep you safe.*

Better his blood than mine.

Using both hands, I let out a cry and brought the knife down.

Emerson Charles let out a roar and spun. His flaming arm hit my shoulder with such force he knocked me sideways. My left hip crashed into a stainless steel table, and my vision started to turn black.

Not exactly the safety I'd been expecting.

*Pyper. Hang on, sweetheart.*

That voice. A tiny ball of joy formed in the middle of my chest. Happiness. Comfort. Familiarity. I knew her.

*Come on, my girl. Open your eyes.*

The chill from the cold hard concrete floor seeped into my bones, and I suddenly remembered where I was and why. My lids fluttered, and I squinted up at the figure hovering over me.

She had raven-black hair and deep blue, wide-set eyes that were filled with so much love I nearly cried. "Mom?"

# Chapter 14

S HE SMILED DOWN at me. *Hi, honey.*

I reached up, trying to press my hand to her rosy cheek, but my hand slipped right through her image, just like it did normally did when I encountered ghostly figures.

She put her hand out, holding it up, and I did the same, simulating that our palms were touching. *You need to get up. People are counting on you.*

I blinked, taking in her healthy glow and her sparkling eyes, the way she used to look before she got sick… before I lost her so many years ago. "Am I dead?"

She chuckled, the sweet tone nearly music to my ears. *Of course not. But if you don't step up and take control of your gifts, your friends are going to get hurt.*

I sat up, rubbing my aching hip. "What gifts? I speak to ghosts. Are you saying I can control who I can talk to and when or something?" The very idea of being able to call on my mom when I wanted was both elating and a little scary. Would I become one of those people who preferred the dead to the living?

She gave me a soft smile. *No. Ghosts have a will of their own as well as limited energy. I think you already know that. And while you can ask for us to appear, it's up to us to decide to answer or not.*

"Then what do you mean take control of my gifts?" My head was pounding, and I was starting wonder if she was really here. Was I hallucinating after my fall?

*You just have to unlock them. A drop of your blood is all it takes.*

I stared at her for a moment, then picked up the knife again and rested the blade against my palm. But I hesitated. If she was a hallucination, then I could be harming myself for no reason… or worse. There was no telling what Emerson could do if he had access to my blood.

*Time is running out.* Mom glanced over her shoulder, and when she turned back, the worry in her eyes had me climbing to my feet. I winced as I put weight on my left foot, but I quickly forgot it when I saw Julius.

He was no longer bound by the thick steel chain, but he was in rough shape. Blood ran from a gash in his head, one arm appeared to be limp as if it had been rendered useless, and he was on one knee, his hand out, producing a magical shield to ward off Emerson's relentless magic that was hammering him with blow after blow. But the shield was failing. After every two or three hits, the shield shattered and Julius produced it again and again and again. The strain was wearing on him. He grunted as he conjured another shield, but this time it only lasted for one attack.

"Goddess. Emerson is going to kill him," I said, covering my mouth to keep from screaming.

*Use the knife, Pyper. You have the power to stop this.* Mom reached out, and even though she was clearly a ghost, I could've sworn I felt her caress my cheek.

"Mom." I raised my hand to cover hers, but I was too late. She vanished.

Noise erupted around me, and I realized while I'd been talking to my mom, I'd been in some sort of a bubble. Now the zing of magic and the clang of tools scattering to the floor filled my senses. But then I heard the low groan of a man, followed by a sinister laugh from Emerson.

"You had enough?" Emerson asked.

Julius stared up at the biker, hatred in his gaze. Then he answered by sending a bolt of magic to the ceiling. The lights flashed once and the entire light fixture came crashing down, barely missing Emerson as the big man dove out of the way, landing on the motorcycle Hale had been dismantling.

Julius slumped, gasping for breath as he wiped the drying blood from his forehead.

But the battle was far from over. Emerson was already on his feet, magic crawling all over his skin as he moved slowly toward Julius.

"You're a dead man," he snarled and touched a chrome tailpipe, instantly incinerating it, leaving only a pile of ashes behind.

Holy hell! Could he do that with anything? Was he going to turn Julius to dust? My hand tightened around the hilt of my knife, and then in one swift motion, I sliced it across my palm. I let out a low hiss from the burn of the blade and waited.

Nothing.

"Dammit!" I cried, tears stinging my eyes. Emerson was closing in on Julius. And even though Julius was back on his feet, magic swirling around him in a protective barrier, I was certain all it would take was one touch and Julius was history. I had to do something. Anything.

Dropping the knife, I reached for a nearby crowbar. But as soon as the knife hit the floor, I noticed the bloodstained tip started to glow. Elation shot through me. It had worked. My blood had unlocked its power.

"Pyper, look out!" Julius shouted from across the room.

In the few seconds it'd taken for me to realize my blood had unleashed something with the knife, so had Emerson Charles. Because while he'd been stalking Julius only moments before, torturing his prey, he was now headed straight for me at full speed.

I dove to the floor, grabbing the knife with my cut hand. The moment my fingers wrapped around the hilt, heat shot through my veins and the pain in my hip and hand vanished. Energy strummed through me, making me feel invincible.

I jumped to my feet, the knife feeling as if it were just another appendage, as if it had always been there in my hand. And when Emerson Charles lunged for me, this time I plunged the knife straight into his chest. The biker froze, and all the magic coating his body vanished. His eyes rolled into the back of his head as he went down in a heap at my feet.

"Oh my god!" I cried and let go of the knife. My entire body shook uncontrollably. Magic still coated the handle, illuminating the man's expressionless face in the fading early-evening light. "I killed him!"

"No," Julius said, limping toward me. He looked like he'd been to hell and back, his blood coating his face and shirt and exhaustion lining his pale face. "You didn't. He's only neutralized." He pointed to the knife, still lodged in Emerson's chest. "Look at it. There's no blood."

"But—Whoa." Julius was right. There wasn't so much as a drop of blood anywhere. In fact, his shirt wasn't torn or bunched in any way from the penetration of the knife. I bent down to really study the dagger. There was no sign of the blade, just the hilt pressed against his shirt. I wrapped my hand around the glowing knife and gently tugged. The knife slid smoothly out of the big man, leaving zero evidence of a stab wound. I gently pressed against his chest, finding nothing but a cotton T-shirt and unbroken skin.

A low rumble came from Emerson just before his hand shot up and gripped me by the neck, squeezing so hard he silenced my startled cry.

He started to mutter something that sounded suspiciously like Latin. A spell. He was calling up his magic.

I didn't hesitate and once more plunged the knife into his chest. His hand fell away, and the biker went limp as I fell back onto my butt and rubbed at my sore throat.

"That's... incredible," Julius said.

I glanced over at my battered boyfriend, then at the motionless witch lying in front of me, and then turned to check on Hale. He was pressed up against the garage wall, wearing only his pink boy shorts and black socks, clutching an oversized wrench. His eyes were wide with shock and his mouth hung open.

"Are you all right?" I asked him.

He nodded slowly, then glanced down at himself, dropped the wrench, and hastily tried to cover his man-junk with both hands.

I shook my head in disbelief. The man had almost gone up in a fiery inferno, witnessed a magical showdown to end all showdowns, and still found the energy to be worried someone was looking at him in his questionable fashion choice? I ignored his lack of clothing and eyed his legs, wincing at the blisters already forming. "You're going to need medical attention."

He nodded again.

"Soon. You might want to try to find some clothes before the ambulance gets here."

"No." He swallowed thickly as he forced the words out. It appeared whatever I'd done to Emerson had neutralized the spell he'd put on Hale. "No ambulance. I'll go to the emergency room."

"Hale—" Too late. The man was already hobbling down the gravel lane toward a white truck parked behind the office. "Why did he stay during the magical fight?" I asked Julius. "If his truck was here the entire time…"

"I'm guessing he was either compelled to stay here by Emerson or he was too afraid," Julius said. "It seems obvious Emerson was forcing him to work for him. We just don't know how or why."

"Yeah. Makes sense." But nothing else did. Not yet anyway.

Julius put his arm around me and pulled me in close. He pressed his warm lips to my temple and whispered, "You saved me."

I turned into him, burying my face against his chest. "No. It was Avrilla. If she hadn't given me the knife…"

"Pyper," he said and pulled away from me slightly. "Your magic neutralized him. You saved me and Hale."

"But I don't have magic," I insisted. "Or at least not any that I can tap. It was the knife. And when we were on the ship it was Vienna Vox's magic. I appear to just be a conduit."

"I don't think so." Julius peered over my shoulder at Emerson's lifeless body. "Otherwise any old blood would have worked on that knife."

I wasn't sure what to make of that. However, my mother had shown up and said I just needed to unlock my power. Did that mean I had magic I could tap, or would it forever be locked in the knife? I wasn't exactly sure if I wanted to find out. At least not right at the moment. "Shouldn't you call someone? Like the council?"

Julius let out a sigh. "Yeah. Let's hope they send someone this time, because I don't know how we're going to haul him in on my bike."

While Julius dialed, I studied Emerson Charles. He was sprawled on the ground, arms and legs bent at unnatural angles while his eyes were wide open, staring at nothing. If it hadn't been for his chest rising and falling with each breath, it would be hard to convince me he wasn't dead. I moved over and nudged a hand with the tip of my boot.

Nothing.

Kneeling, I placed my hand directly over the left side of his chest and nearly yanked it back when I felt the steady strum of his heart. But still there was no movement, no magic coating his body, and nothing to indicate he wasn't totally incapacitated.

Good. Because if there was ever a time to search his property, now was it. Without so much as a whisper of guilt, I rummaged through the man's front pockets until my fingers closed around his keys. No doubt one of them would open his office. If he was stupid enough to leave any records around that led to either Bo or Mia, I was going to find them.

Mentally and physically exhausted, I tightened my grip

around the keys and started down the gravel lane back toward the office.

"Pyper!" Julius called.

I turned and glanced over my shoulder to find him waving frantically.

"Hurry. It's the knife."

A jolt of adrenaline shot through me and I ran flat out back into the garage. The knife had turned electric blue and was slowly but surely working its way out of the Emerson Charles's chest.

"What the hell?" I asked and moved closer. Emerson blinked up at me, his eyes glittering with hatred. But when he moved his mouth, no sound came out. "Oh God. He's waking up."

Julius, still on the phone, relayed the situation to the council member, but I'd stopped listening to him. The warm magic I'd felt earlier started to strum through my veins, and my hand itched to reach for the knife. There was a strange pull that connected me with the object.

"You need to reconnect with the knife," Julius said from behind me. "It's your magic keeping him neutralized."

My magic. I could feel it pulsing everywhere. My skin heated and I felt invincible. Was this what it was like to be Jade? The high was incredible... and also terrifying. No one should have so much power over another person.

"You... are a dead witch... walking," Emerson forced out between cracked lips.

Anger made my mind buzz, and all other thoughts vanished as I knelt down and whispered. "You first."

Then I grabbed the hilt of the knife and slammed it back

into his chest, twisting it for good measure.

The electric-blue magic that had been coating the hilt poured over him, encasing him in a thin sheet of ice-like magic. His limbs stiffened, leaving him with one arm slightly raised while his other hand lay mere inches from the hilt of the knife. He was frozen once again, unable to move anything... except this time he was conscious as he glared up at me.

I stared down into his dark eyes and felt nothing but satisfaction.

# Chapter 15

"THE COUNCIL ISN'T coming," Julius said.

I nodded from my place on the concrete floor. Nothing they did surprised me. Either they were the most incompetent magical law enforcement department ever, or the world was imploding and they were severely understaffed. Right then I was going for incompetent. But likely the truth was somewhere in the middle. "If we manage to get him back to the council, is there someone there to deal with him?"

He nodded. "Yes."

"All right." I picked up my phone and dialed Jade.

"We're almost to Mayhem. Where do you want us to meet you?" she asked by way of greeting.

I rattled off the address, then added, "And Jade?"

"Yeah?"

"Get here as soon as you can. We have a situation."

✧   ✧   ✧

"YOU'RE SAYING YOU did this?" Jade asked me as she knelt beside Emerson Charles, inspecting the knife.

I wrapped my arms around myself, suddenly feeling very exposed and vulnerable.

"How?" Kane, my best friend and her husband, draped an arm around my shoulder, pulling me in for a sideways hug.

I glanced up at him and had to blink back the tears that stung my eyes. He'd been my person, my pseudobrother, for so long that just seeing him walk into the garage had brought on a well of emotion. I swallowed. Hard. Then cleared my throat. "Apparently my blood unleashed the magic from the knife."

Jade turned, her long strawberry-blond hair falling over one eye. But there was no missing the alarm in her expression. "It's blood magic?"

"Well, yeah, I guess," I said hesitantly, an ache forming in my gut. Blood magic was dangerous, and despite knowing the entire time the knife required blood to unleash its power, it hadn't even occurred to me to question the safety of the magical blade. I'd needed it and would use it again if I had to, but being affiliated with dark magic wasn't something I was happy about.

"It's not what you're thinking," Julius quickly clarified.

All three of us turned in unison, giving Julius our undivided attention.

"That knife only worked when it came in contact with Pyper's blood. For some reason, once her blood touched the blade, it unlocked her magic. But Emerson's blood didn't do it. And the knife stops working if she gets too far away. It's as if it's made for her and only her."

Jade frowned. "And you said a ghost witch gave it to you?"

"Yes. My mom showed up too."

Jade's eyes widened, and Kane's grip around my shoulder tightened.

"What did she say?" Jade asked.

I relayed the short conversation we'd shared and then

shrugged. "She wasn't here for very long."

"Wow." Jade nodded. "It does sound like it was made just for you. But why?"

"That's the real question, isn't it?" Julius added. "But unless we find Avrilla again, I'm not sure we're going to get the answer. And right now, we have other issues to deal with." He waved at the still-incapacitated biker. "We need to get him to the council, and we still have to find Bo and Mia."

"I can take him," Kane said, resting his hand on the dagger strapped to his side. He was a demon hunter and never left home without it. And even though it was specifically for battling demons, it was a useful tool in combating all kinds of magic.

"Not alone. You need backup." Jade turned to Julius. "You pretty much have to go, right?"

Julius met my gaze, and after a moment, he nodded.

I slipped out of Kane's brotherly embrace and went to Julius's side. He needed healing herbs, a shower, and a change of clothes. Not to mention a good night's sleep and a hot meal. "You should stay with Jade. It makes sense that I go. As long as I'm with him and the knife stays buried in his chest, there's no chance of another altercation."

"You don't know that." Julius slipped his hand around mine and squeezed lightly. "The magic could wear off any minute. Until we know more about this knife and what it means for you, we can't assume anything."

"He's right," Jade said. "We can't risk what we don't know." Then she dug around in her bag and produced a small metal tin. "Here." She handed the metal container to Julius. "You'll find turmeric healing lozenges in there along with a variety of teas that will help with pain reduction and stimulate healing."

"So you're saying Kane and Julius are going to take Emerson to the council while we stay here?" I asked her, trying to fight the anxiety crawling up the back of my neck. The thought of sending the only two men in my life I'd ever loved off with the one who had just tried to kill Julius was too much.

"I'm not sure we have a choice," Jade said softly. "We could all go, but what about this young man you're worried about? Or Mia? Five years is a long time to be held captive. Do you want to put the search on hold while we deal with this guy?"

"He could be the answer to where they both are," I said. "And the fastest path to finding them both."

Jade stared at the incapacitated biker. She narrowed her eyes, then stalked over to him, reached down, and yanked the knife out of his chest.

His eyes bulged as he sucked in a large gasp of breath.

"Whoa! Jade, I don't think—"

Jade held up a hand to stop me. "Where are Bo and Mia?" she demanded, her hands on her hips.

He pushed himself up, gripping the middle of his unmarred chest. "What?" He blinked, then zeroed in on me, his eyes shooting daggers. "You are going to wish you'd never been born when I get my hands on you."

Jade kicked him in the gut, knocking him over, and held him down with one foot. "Right now you have a bigger problem, buddy."

He snarled up at her. "You think you can take me?" Reaching up with one hand, he streamed magic from his palm, but it petered out instantly.

Jade raised one skeptical eyebrow. "Looks like any one of us could take you right now."

He growled and grasped her ankle, but even as he tried to twist to cause her to lose her balance, she shot a bolt of her white magic straight into his chest at the exact spot I'd plunged the magical knife. He cried out and let go, lying there panting while we all stared at him.

"Try something like that again and the next time, I'll take an eye out. Got it?" She wouldn't. I knew her better than that. Not unless she had no other choice. But there was no point in letting him believe otherwise.

He scowled but didn't answer her.

"Pyper." She held the knife out to me. "I think you're going to want this."

The blue ice-magic that had coated Emerson still shimmered along the knife, but it didn't seem to bother Jade. However, the moment I wrapped my fingers around the hilt, that warm jolt of magic shot into my arm and spread through my body, reenergizing me. All the fatigue and weariness vanished.

I held the knife out, inspecting it. The magic was gone and it looked just as mundane as it had when I'd stuffed it into my pocket earlier that morning.

Jade tilted her head to the side, contemplating. A slow smile spread over her face. "Pyper, my friend, it looks like you've just joined our little magical club. Because there's no doubt the power contained in that knife is bound to you. If it wasn't, I would've absorbed it when I grabbed it."

"But why?" I asked.

"That's a question we'll answer later. Right at this moment, this creepster is going to tell us what he did with Mia." She nudged him with her foot. "Right, dillweed?"

"I don't know what you're talking about," Emerson said, his words clipped and full of menace. "My brother already paid the ultimate price for the disappearance of that meddlesome witch. Why the hell would I know where she is? Last I heard, the authorities pronounced her dead."

"But he says she's alive," I countered. "And don't pretend to not know what I'm talking about. You banished his ghost earlier right here in this garage."

Emerson pushed himself up to a sitting position and gritted his teeth. "That ghost is not my brother."

"What's that supposed to mean?" I demanded.

"Exactly what I said. When those pieces of shit shot him, he died and whatever came back in his place is delusional. You can't trust anything he says."

Julius and I shared a glance. He shook his head slightly. I'd come across my share of crazy ghosts before. The longer they were in ghost form, the more likely it was for them to start losing their minds. But Sterling hadn't been gone that long. Just a few years, and he appeared perfectly sane to me.

"Seems like the man who just tried to obliterate my friends is the one we can't really trust," Jade said, glaring at him. "Not to mention the black hole of toxic energy wafting off you. Now, I'm going to give you five seconds to tell us where Bo is and what you know about Mia or you're going to find yourself trussed up and presented to the council with a big red bow."

His eyes darted between me and Jade, then to Julius before landing on Kane. "And who are you? Her manservant?"

Kane chuckled. "Sometimes. But right now I'm here just to

watch the show. There's nothing sexier than watching my girl kick a dickhead in the balls."

"One…" Jade held a finger up as she started to count.

"Shit." The biker started lumbering to his feet. His movements were slow and deliberate, though not as if he was in pain. More like he was just watching us carefully. Whatever my knife had done to him before, it didn't seem like the magic had left much of a lasting effect.

"Two." She waved her first two fingers in air.

"Better start talking," Kane said, moving his hand to the dagger on his hip.

"Three." Jade took a step forward.

"He's not going to say anything," Julius added.

I had to agree. Emerson's eyes were now darting around the garage as if he was contemplating some way of escape. It was smart on his part, because there was no way we were going to let him go.

"Four." Static electricity started to lift Jade's strawberry-blond hair, and her emerald-green eyes flashed. My body buzzed, and the unfamiliar yet intoxicating magic I was still getting used to coursed through me. Every molecule of my being was on high alert, ready to strike at any moment.

Emerson's gaze swept over her, and then I felt rather than saw the torrent of magic rise within him. Power shot down my arm and straight back into the dagger, and then on instinct, I flung the blade right at him. It spun through the air, tip over hilt, and landed perfectly, once again in his chest, as if I'd been expertly trained in knife throwing.

The magic he'd called up vanished instantly, and the big man fell backward, landing flat on his back.

Everyone was silent for a moment. Then Kane let out a low whistle, and Julius began a slow clap.

"Wow," Jade said, awe in her tone. "That was... impressive."

I shrugged. "All I did was throw a knife."

"Hardly." Jade beamed at me, her eyes no longer flashing and her hair once again back to normal. "You felt him call up his magic and neutralized him even before I could. Damn, I sure am glad you're on my team."

"How did you know that?" I asked her. "I mean about knowing I felt his magic."

She shrugged. "Empath."

"Of course." There was no need for any other explanation. Reading other peoples' energy was her gift. Certainly she'd felt my reaction to him, and that's all she'd needed.

"You also felt mine." A teasing smile claimed Jade's lips as she added, "But thanks for refraining from stabbing me in the heart." She waved a hand at Emerson. "Lying flat out on a greasy concrete floor doesn't look like a ton of fun."

"You're welcome," I said quietly. And despite my friends' obvious delight at my new abilities, a pit of unease settled in my stomach. Being a medium was one thing. And there was no doubt excelling at knife throwing was pretty badass. But if I'd learned anything in the past few years, possessing powerful magic meant one thing: trouble.

# Chapter 16

"WE'LL BE BACK later tonight," Julius said, opening the passenger-side door of Kane's new Lexus SUV. Emerson was in the cargo hold in the back, his hands, feet, and mouth magically bound. Once I'd removed my knife, Jade hadn't held back on magically binding him. There was no way he was going anywhere before the council witches lifted the spell.

I wrapped my arms around Julius and pressed my head to his chest, not wanting to let go. "Call me if you learn anything new."

"You know I will." He rested his chin on the top of my head. "And you take care of the bike. No riding in the rain. And no drag racing, no matter who challenges you."

I pulled back and opened my mouth in mock indignation. "No drag racing? You're no fun."

He gave me a smirk. "That's not what you said this morning."

I laughed. "Fair enough. Go hand that jackass off to the council and hurry back. I have plans for you later."

"Plans that include traipsing through the bayou and putting the smackdown on anyone else involved in Mia's kidnapping?"

"Something like that." I reached up and pressed my lips to his, trying to ignore the pang in my chest. And even though I knew he'd be perfectly fine—in his own way, Julius was just as powerful as Jade—there was something inside me that ached with the thought of being separated from him, if only for a short time. It unsettled me.

"What's wrong?" he asked, eyeing me when we broke apart.

Crap. He'd noticed my turmoil. I forced a smile. "You mean besides Bo and Mia?"

"Yes. I know you're amped up about finding them both, but there's something else. What is it?"

I sighed and pressed my hand to his chest, wanting to be connected to him. "Just unsettled after what happened back there. It's not every day a girl finds out she has supernatural powers. I'll be fine. Jade's here to protect me… or to keep me from blowing myself up."

His eyes searched mine. "If you want me to stay—"

"No." I held a hand up. "You have a job to do. Go do it. I'll be here when you get back."

"You'd better be." With one last kiss on my cheek, he gingerly climbed into the SUV.

"Make sure you take those herbs Jade gave you. Okay?"

He held up the metal tin. "Will do. I'll be as good as knew next time you see me."

"Good." I waved as Kane pulled out of the parking lot, leaving Jade and me behind. I turned to her. "Ready?"

She grinned. "Always."

I climbed on the bike, secured my helmet, and after she did the same, I kicked the bike to life. "Hold on!" I called over my shoulder.

The second her hands came around my waist, I put the bike in gear and flew down the highway.

✧ ✧ ✧

Before we'd loaded Emerson into the SUV, Jade and I had searched his office building but found nothing out of the ordinary. There had been stacks of invoices and customer receipts on his desk. The only oddity was the sheer number of parts ordered and sold. Unless they were selling their inventory online through eBay, there was no way a town as small as Twin Forks could support that kind of volume.

"The shop has to be a front for something else. Most likely drugs," I said to Jade as we walked up to the inn's front door. "And I'd bet my last dollar they are forcing Bo to be a part of it."

"That's possible." Jade stared at the inn, frowning.

"What?" I asked, glancing around for anything unusual or out of place. But the sun had set and the only thing I could make out was the pathway, which was lined with a half dozen garden lights.

"There's unusual energy coming from inside the house."

I paused midstep. "What does that mean… unusual?" If we walked through the front door, were we going to end up in another magical showdown? Goddess, I hoped not. Besides being exhausted, all I wanted was one of Moxie's warm muffins and a fresh cup of coffee.

She shook her head, her brows pinched. "I don't know. It's like a dark cloud is hovering overhead. Not evil, just… unsettled."

"Well, that's reassuring," I said, doing nothing to hide the sarcasm in my tone.

She gave me an apologetic smile. "Sorry. I just can't put my finger on what's bothering me. Something's off."

"Okay." I closed my fingers around my dagger, comforted by the magic that suddenly sprang to life.

"Do you feel it?" Jade asked. "The energy in the house, I mean."

That was a good question. Could I? I'd felt Jade's magic and Emerson's back at the Twin Forks garage. Could I tap into other energy? I closed my eyes and concentrated on Jade. My pulse rate seemed to speed up slightly, and that rush of magic intensified. I definitely could sense her magical energy. But what about the house? I took a few deep breaths and focused on the door.

Nothing.

Closing my eyes, I recalled the entry, the wooden stairs, and the adjacent living room area. My pulse didn't speed up, but there was something there. Something that felt a lot like queasiness.

"Um, if what you feel makes you want to heave, then yes. I feel it." My eyes popped open, and the minute I focused on Jade, the queasiness dissipated.

"Heave?" she asked. "No. But it does make my skin itch a little. Whatever it is, we just need to be prepared."

"So far we've been in more danger of walking in on inappropriate role play."

"Really?" Jade laughed.

I chuckled with her. "Really. But they've been fighting the past few days, so you might be spared."

The entry was dark except for one dim wall light. Low

murmurs came from the living room, and before we clambered up the stairs, I poked my head in on Hale and Moxie.

The pair sat on the couch, Moxie draped over Hale's lap, their heads bent as they spoke quietly. He was dressed in a clean T-shirt and loose shorts while she wore leggings and a tunic. I glanced down at Hale's exposed legs and winced. They were angry and marked with blisters. He should've gone straight to the hospital for medical attention.

"Pyper," Moxie called over Hale's shoulder. "Good, you're here."

"We didn't mean to interrupt," I said, already backing out of the room. "I just wanted to make sure Hale got home safely."

"Yes, thanks to you apparently." She smiled, but her eyes were tired as she waved me forward. "Can we talk to you for a minute?"

"Sure." I nodded for Jade to follow me into the living room. Moxie's lavender scent was stronger than usual, making my nose itch, and I wondered how Hale managed to sit right next to her.

After I introduced Jade, we sat opposite them in a pair of matching club chairs. And just as I was about to ask what this was all about, Stella came bounding into the room, yapping. Moxie's cat let out a yowl and took off into the adjoining office. The little dog made a beeline right for me and launched herself into my lap. I picked her up and snuggled her against my shoulder, soothed by the weight of her small body against mine.

Hale cleared his throat, and when I glanced up, he met my gaze head on. "Thank you for what you did today."

I gave a half shrug. "I didn't do anything anyone else wouldn't have done in my position."

He let out a humorless laugh. "Not in this town. No one

stands up to Emerson Charles."

"No one?" Jade asked, curiously. "Why is that exactly? Are there no other witches around who are willing to engage him?"

"There were," Hale admitted. "But after everything went down with Sterling and Mia, Emerson went on a morality kick. He started spewing stuff about family and loyalty and how the people of this town needed to come together to rise above all the evil that lurks out there. Anyone who dared use their magic couldn't be trusted and ultimately was ostracized. He made the claim that Sterling and Mia were experimenting too much with their powers and that Sterling accidently killed her. And while he's never come out and said that Sterling got what he deserved, it's been implied many times over."

"So what happened to the other witches in town?" I asked, trying to piece together what he was telling me.

"They're either working for Emerson, left town, or were forced out," Moxie said.

"And the Swamp Witch shop? Is the proprietor an actual witch, or…?"

Hale shook his head. "She just sells novelty stuff. Once everyone else with any sort of magic disappeared from Mayhem, Emerson started showing his true colors. He threatens, bribes, blackmails, and spells people to do his bidding."

"That's the only reason Hale was working for him," Moxie said softly. "He couldn't afford for—"

"Moxie, no!" Hale frowned and shook his head.

"How are we ever going to get out of this situation if we don't tell someone?" she asked, hastily pushing her unwieldy, curly hair out of the way.

"We'll be fine. I'll handle it," he muttered and glanced

away.

Jade and I shared a glance. She mouthed, *Guilt. Lots of guilt* and pointed at Hale. I didn't need to be an empath to figure that out.

"I don't know what your role was at the Emerson's garage, but I promise you can trust us," I said, trying to sound reassuring.

"Really? Doesn't your boyfriend work for the Witches' Council?" Hale asked, his eyes narrowed in challenge.

"Well, yes, but neither of us do, and he's not here right now." Stella lifted her head and started to growl for no apparent reason. I ran my hand over her head, calming the little troublemaker. "Besides, unless you have magical abilities, then they don't have any jurisdiction over you."

He let out a huff of humorless laughter. "That's the bitch of it. I am a witch, though I never wanted to be one. Never wanted to cast spells or deal with the darkness that ultimately comes along with being cursed with power."

I couldn't say I blamed him. In fact, learning that I had magic, even if it was attached to the dagger, had given me pause. The terrible things I'd seen Jade have to deal with over the past few years were enough to make anyone walk away from all things magic. Most didn't because the power surge was too intoxicating. If he'd managed it, he was stronger than I was. Still, something was bothering me about his statement. "If you have magic, why didn't you fight back when Emerson attacked you?"

Hale opened his mouth to speak, but no words came out. Then he let out a groan of frustration and shook his head, his fists clenched.

Moxie's body tensed, and she let out an exaggerated sigh. "Dammit. Not again. He won't be able to talk for days now."

"What? Why?" Jade leaned forward, her elbows on her knees as she studied him. "What just happened there?"

Hale gently pushed Moxie off him and stood. He didn't look back as he limped into the next room.

Moxie bit her bottom lip, then she grimaced and shook her head. "I'm not sure if this is a good idea, but I'm going to tell you what I know and pray it doesn't come back to bite Hale in the butt. Can I really trust you, two?"

"Yes," we both said in unison.

Jade smiled at me, then turned her attention to Moxie. "You don't know me, so I can understand the apprehension, but let me lay my background out for you. I'm a white witch, leader of the New Orleans coven. I don't work for the council, but a couple of my coven members do. I don't use black magic. Or at least never intentionally. There have been a few close calls when my friends or myself have been in mortal danger. My husband is a demon hunter. Neither of us would dream of using our powers against anyone else for personal gain. My mission here is to help Pyper find Mia and now Bo, who appears to be missing. If Hale is in trouble, I'll do everything in my power to help him out too. All you need to do is give me a chance."

My heart swelled as I listened to my friend. She didn't have to put herself on the line to help strangers, but there she was, stepping up just as she always did. Remarkable didn't even begin to describe her.

"And you?" Moxie asked me. "Why are you getting involved in a five-year-old kidnapping of someone you've never even met?"

It was on the tip of my tongue to answer, *Why wouldn't I?* But her question deserved better than that. "I don't want to be cliché and say something like 'with great power comes great responsibility,' because that sounds like a BS answer and not the whole truth. But I'm not sure how else to put it. Most people don't see ghosts, but I do. And when one seeks me out with information that can help someone, I can't just ignore it. I know what it's like to be held captive by evil, and I won't stand by and let it happen to someone else. For me, it's personal."

She let my words sink in for a moment, then she nodded. "I can see that. Okay, what I'm about to tell you has to stay between us. If Emerson Charles is released and he finds out I've told you any of this, Hale's a dead man. Understood?"

"Your secret is safe with us," I said while Jade nodded.

"Okay then." She sucked in a breath. "Hale pledged an oath of fealty to Emerson Charles, just like all his bikers have. And when he did, a spell was cast that rendered him unable to use his magic specifically against Emerson or spill any of Emerson's secrets. In fact, he can only use magic when Emerson orders him to."

"And?" I prompted, knowing there had to be more. Otherwise they wouldn't have been worried about the council.

Her expression turned steely as she forced out, "Emerson Charles runs an illegal chop shop. Did you know that?"

I shook my head. But it did explain a few things, such as the excess invoices in his office. He had to have some sort of paper trail for the accountants if he was banking illegal sales.

"I'm not surprised," she added. "Because then you'd likely already know that Hale is his right-hand man."

# Chapter 17

"WHAT?" I ASKED, my eyes widening as a wave of shock rolled over me. That was the last thing I was expecting her to say. "He's in business with Emerson Charles?"

"I wouldn't say in business exactly, but without Hale, it would be a lot harder. You see, Hale is gifted at memory modification. For the past four years, his job has been to make the victims believe they sold their bikes to Twin Forks Cycles. In exchange for his 'obedience,' Hale was allowed to maintain a certain portion of his freedom, which basically meant he didn't have to live at the Twin Forks compound like most of the rest of them do. Emerson Charles is a dictator."

They had a compound? Was that where Bo was? Had he been under Emerson's spell as well? My stomach turned at the thought of the young man being exploited by his so-called guardian. "It sounds like you're implying Hale was an unwilling participant."

"Damn straight he is!" She sat up straight and pointed toward the door. "Do you think that sweet man would ever do such a thing if he had a choice?"

"No, that's not my impression of him," I said.

She slumped and tears welled in her dark eyes. "It's been

terrible. Hale donates as much of the money as he can to youth programs. We didn't know what else to do."

Jade stood and moved over to the couch to sit next to Moxie. She gently took the woman's hand in hers, and although I didn't doubt Jade was trying to comfort her, I suspected she also wanted a better read on the woman's emotions. "Four years is a long time. Didn't anyone ever question why they sold their bikes? Not even after the spells wore off?"

She shook her head. "Not once. Part of the scam included taking the victim back to the Twin Forks lair, where he was drugged and robbed of any cash on his person. In the morning, he wakes up in some obscure motel with memories of hooking up with one of the biker babes and thinking he spent all his cash on her while he partied like a rock star. If and when the spell loses its punch, their memories are so vague and confused, they don't really know what happened."

"Holy balls," I breathed. "Emerson is a human cockroach."

Moxie nodded and wiped the tears from her cheeks. Her eyes were sunken and shadowed as if she hadn't slept in days. "Now that Emerson is at least temporarily incarcerated, we've made a decision. We're leaving town."

"Why now?" I asked. "As opposed to when this all started?"

She snorted in frustration. "I asked Hale the same thing earlier today. He said it's because Emerson would've come after us. But now that Emerson has attacked him, he's willing to risk it." Standing, she smoothed her tunic. "We're leaving tonight while we still can."

"Tonight?" It was already after nine. Finding another place to stay was going to be difficult at best, especially with a rambunctious shih tzu. "Okay, let me grab our bags and we'll get out of your way."

"No, no," she said, shaking her head. "You can stay here as long as you like. The utilities are paid through the end of the month. Don't let us put you out on the street."

"That's kind of you," I said, breathing a sigh of relief.

"Do you know where you'll go?" Jade asked, her head tilted to one side as she looked up at the woman.

Moxie shrugged. "North maybe? Definitely out of state. Maybe out of the country. As far as we can get before Emerson is released."

I studied the woman standing in front of us. She was so different than the one I'd met a few days ago when we'd checked in. Before, she'd been happy, bubbly, full of mischief and life as she planned her dates with Hale. But tonight she was just tired. Worn out and disillusioned.

Jade stood and turned to Moxie, her expression filled with curiosity. "Can I ask you one more thing?"

"Uh, sure." Moxie glanced over her shoulder as if looking for Hale. But when she didn't see him, she returned her attention to Jade.

"If Emerson spelled Hale in order to keep him from talking about their arrangement, how is that you know all this?"

Moxie let out a mocking laugh. "Emerson Charles is many things, but discreet is not one of them. Not when he's trying to get a woman into bed anyway. Apparently he thought that informing me he controls my boyfriend would be a turn-on."

"You mean he came on to you?" I asked, wondering how it was possible to harbor so much loathing for one human being.

"Yes. And he still does. Pretty much every chance he gets." She reached behind the desk and picked up a familiar plastic bin. The top was missing, and inside I spied no less than a dozen brightly colored adult toys. When she noticed me staring, her tight smile vanished, replace by a mischievous one. "Now that we're getting out of this town, I have big plans to help Hale get his groove back." Then she winked and disappeared to go pack.

✧   ✧   ✧

JADE AND I stood in front of the inn, watching Hale and Moxie drive off into the night. We were silent until the red taillights disappeared around a corner.

"Are you all right?" I asked her.

She didn't say anything at first, then she nodded. "Fine. Just frustrated. I'll take a few healing herbs and be good as new."

She'd spent the past twenty minutes trying to break the curse Emerson had laid on Hale. But all she'd managed to accomplish was plaguing herself with a pounding headache. The result suggested that Emerson had used black magic.

I stared down the street once more and prayed Hale and Moxie would find some peace. Meanwhile, we had a teenager to find.

"Ready to start that finding spell?" I asked her.

She rummaged around in her small bag and then popped two herbal pills. "I'm ready when you are. Just as long as you still have his hat."

I walked over to the Harley and retrieved the hat from one of the saddlebags. Brandishing it in the air, I said, "Got it."

"Perfect. Now all we need is a circle. Or at least somewhere we can tap earth energy."

"I don't know about a circle, but I think I have somewhere

that might work. Follow me." I led Jade through the old house, stopping briefly to scratch Stella behind the ears, and then out into the backyard. I was right—there wasn't a circle, but there was a magnificent cypress tree. I walked over to the gentle giant, spread my arms wide, and asked, "Will this do?"

*For what? A close encounter of the woman kind?* Ida May materialized right next to the tree. *Is Julius already letting you down? That's got to be hard... Err, not exactly hard if he's letting you down, right? What a bummer. But he is over a hundred years old. You know what they say happens to older men. They need a lot more fluffing.*

"Ida May! Jeez. No. We're doing a finding spell."

"Hello, Ida May," Jade called out even though she couldn't see or communicate with her.

*Tell Shortcake I said hey.* Ida May referred to Kane's nickname for Jade. She floated back and forth, her dark hair drifting as if it were caught in the mild breeze. How was she doing that?

"She says hey," I said automatically.

An amused smile claimed Jade's lips. "Even though I can't see or hear Ida May, the expression on your face while you're talking to her is priceless. I swear the pair of you are like an old married couple."

"Yeah, and one of us doesn't even have the option of killing the other," I quipped.

Jade nodded knowingly. "That's probably a good thing."

"Maybe." I rolled my eyes. "But enough about Ida May. Let's get on with it. I don't want Bo left in the club's hands for any longer than necessary."

Jade glanced around, studying the space. Her eyes narrowed

as she peered through the darkness. "You sure this can't wait until tomorrow morning?"

I bit my lower lip. "I'd rather not. You know how awful it is to be trapped against your will."

"Yeah, okay. But I might need some help with the circle. I'm not sure I'm strong enough to hold it and cast the spell."

*Pick me! Pick me!* Ida May chanted into my ear.

I waved a hand. "Enough, Ida May. I heard you."

"What does she want now?" Jade asked, humor lacing her tone. Like me, she had a soft spot for the ghost's antics.

"To join the circle when we do the finding spell." I rolled my eyes. As a ghost, it was all Ida May could do just to stay present, let alone be an anchor for a spelling circle.

*Yes! I always wanted to conjure up a hot man to do my bidding.* She spun in an elated circle, her arms spread wide and her head tilted back.

I turned to Jade. "Looks like she's participating whether we like it or not."

Jade shrugged. "I was referring to you when I said I'd need help. But Ida May can join too. What's the worst thing she can do?"

"Make my ears bleed?"

*Oh, shut it*, Ida May said. *You know you love me. I'm the best thing that's happened to Bourbon Street since Prohibition ended.*

I laughed and shook my head. It was hard to stay annoyed when she was so entertaining.

"Over here." Jade walked around a small patch of grass to the right of the old tree. "It's fortified by the roots of the tree, and if I'm not mistaken has been used for casting spells before. There's a faint trace of magical energy, as if a witch once called this place home."

I recalled what Moxie had said about Mia and how she was a witch. "Mia and Moxie were close. It's possible she did spell work here."

Jade's eyes sparkled with interest. "Really? That could work in our favor. If I could tap into her residual magic, that could form a connection, a bond that would make finding her that much easier."

"You can do that?" I asked, my eyebrows raised.

*Jade can do anything,* Ida May said in a singsong voice. *Haven't you been paying attention?*

I ignored the ghost, keeping my attention fixed on Jade.

"Maybe." She pulled a jar of salt out of her bag, hastily laid a salt circle, then placed a white candle in the middle. After eyeing her handiwork, she took her place on what would be the northernmost point of the makeshift circle. "It doesn't hurt to try."

Right. I followed, standing opposite her on the southern end, and added, "Famous last words."

# Chapter 18

J ADE RAISED HER hands skyward. "Goddess of the earth, hear my call."

A low rumbling sounded overhead, and Jade's lips curved into a pleased smile. She was getting better at this.

"We ask you to let us share in your gifts, to connect us to the earth, to let us transcend our physical state."

A bolt of lightning skittered across the sky at the same time the makeshift circle lit up beneath our feet. A surge of magical energy slammed into me, and instead of feeling consumed by it as I usually did, it fortified me, coaxed out the latent power buried within my being, and made me feel strong. Instead of just being a conduit for the magic, I could help control it, back Jade up in any of the spells she cast. I raised my arms to the side, filling up on the magic, ready to do my part for the coming spell.

*Can someone turn the heat down please?* Ida May complained, fanning herself. *It's like someone left the door to hell open.*

"What do you mean—" I was cut off when Ida May started to scream. "Jade! It's Ida May. She's—"

The screaming stopped abruptly as Ida May suddenly materialized in human form. She glanced down at herself, smiled, and then started to laugh.

"Um, that isn't exactly what I was expecting," Jade said. The circle was still lit up with magic, but Jade had lowered her arms and the power she'd been building to start the finding spell began to fade.

"I love being human," Ida May said between bouts of giggles.

"Who doesn't?" I said. This wasn't the first time Ida May had been spelled into human form. But the other times we'd thought it was a specific ability of the witch who'd spelled her. This implied that Ida May had some affinity for magic since Jade hadn't actually cast a spell on her.

"Oh my *gawd*. What is that smell?" Ida May asked.

I raised my head and sniffed the air. "Swamp water?"

"Yes!" Her face lit up with pleasure. "It reminds me of my youth. Skinny-dipping with the Roth boys, stealing moonshine, and making out on the docks."

Jade chuckled. "Sounds like some stories for later. Right now we need to get this party started. Pyper? Ready?"

I nodded. "Let's do this."

"Okay then. Here, take this." Jade handed the hat to Ida May. "You hold this. And then when I say so, drip some of the candle wax on it." She indicated the white candle she'd left in the middle of the circle. "Got it?"

"What am I? A simpleton? Of course I've got it. Let's find this guy so I can see if he's my type."

"Ida May." I sighed. "He's only seventeen. Try not to get yourself arrested, will you?"

"Seventeen is a little young, I'll give you that. But sometimes the newbies are the most fun, if you know what I mean." She smirked and fluffed her hair.

"Oh em gee. Not funny," I said, admonishing her.

"Relax! I was joking. Keep your shirt on."

"Words to live by," I mumbled.

Ida May chuckled and moved to the middle of the circle. "Okay, let's get this show started. I don't have all night."

No one knew if she did or didn't, but that didn't matter. I was more than ready to get started. And so was Jade.

She immediately raised her arms out, coaxing the fading magic back to life.

The circle grew brighter than it had before, and the balls of my feet heated with the magical energy she was producing. The power raced through my limbs and coiled in my right palm. That was weird. Most witches used both hands. But mine was twitching, already reaching for the dagger strapped to my waist. Without conscious thought, I wrapped my fingers around the hilt and felt a burst of magic fill me.

Across the circle, Jade's eyes were closed as she chanted the incantation. "From north to east to south to west, find the spirit, reveal its nest. Through brilliance and shadows, with nowhere to hide, reveal the young man we know as Bo, with eyes open wide."

Her words fed the circle, made the magic intensify with every beat of my pulse. It was powerful. Dangerous even. But it didn't scare me. It only made me feel alive.

Jade's eyes popped open, and she stared straight at me. "Visualize Bo. See him in your mind."

I took a deep breath and did as she asked. I imagined him as he was the day we'd gone out on the gator tour, when I'd questioned him about his future. He'd been such a contradiction. Full of cocky confidence and yet already defeated by the world. My heart ached for him and all he must've already gone through while being Emerson's ward.

"From north to south to east to west, light the flame as you see best," Jade called over the wind now whistling through the night.

I opened my eyes, concentrating on the candle beside Ida May's feet. The wind picked up, making her lacy nightgown billow behind her. Ida May tilted her head into the wind, appearing to enjoy the rush of air against her skin. But then all at once the wind stopped, followed by a flash of light in the sky. And when it winked out, the candle flickered in the light breeze.

None of the antics surprised me. There was always a buildup of magic followed by the calm before the storm. The only question was what would happen when Ida May dripped the wax on the hat? Chaos? Or...?

Jade chanted the incantation once more. The magic skittering along the circle shot straight up, encircling us. She raised her arms higher, and with the movement, the candle rose in the air and moved to hover just in front of Ida May. "Pour the wax now!"

For once Ida May did as she was told. Holding the hat out with one hand, she grasped the candle with the other and let the wax drip liberally over the bill.

Upon contact, the beads of wax turned into glowing orbs of light, startling Ida May. She jumped back, releasing the hat, but instead of it falling, the orbs of light danced around it, somehow keeping it levitated.

I watch, completely fascinated as I felt the object pull on the magic I possessed.

"Come on," Jade urged. "Show us where to find Bo."

The light intensified, zooming faster and faster until the hat spun and jerked back and forth within the circle. The light carried it around Ida May, over to Jade, high in the air, and then finally it lowered to the center of the circle, turned until the bill was pointed straight toward me. The breath seemed to vanish from my lungs as I waited, anticipation making me light-headed.

"Help us find Bo," I said.

At my words, the hat barreled forward, hitting me straight in the chest, and fell at my feet. Upon the hat's contact with the earth, the magical walls of the circle vanished and all that was left were the five little light orbs that had previously been beads of wax. They clung to the hat, shining brightly in the moonless night.

"What happened?" I asked, afraid I'd messed something up.

"I think—" Jade started.

"It's waiting for a sacrifice," a deep voice said from out of nowhere.

"Well, hello there, handsome," Ida May crooned.

"Who is that?" Jade asked, glancing around the circle. It was clear she couldn't see our visitor either.

I blinked and watched Ida May stroll across the circle. Tilting her head, she smiled and made the motion of slipping her fingers through someone else's. The magic on the circle shot up again, causing the power in my core to once again pulse as the ghost we'd heard slowly materialized.

"Sterling," I said, noting that besides the missing bike, he looked exactly the same as he had the other two times I'd encountered him. Leather jacket, stubbled jaw, short dark hair.

Tattoos crawled up his neck and covered the backs of his hands.

"Nice." Ida May looked him up and down and deliberately licked her lips. "It's too bad you're ghostly. I could've used a little handling from a man like you tonight."

"Oh goddess," I muttered. "Ida May, keep your hormones in check, will you?"

She scoffed. "Why? What have I got to lose?"

"It's not about you," I said, exasperated. "We're in the middle of a finding spell, and if it doesn't work, we're back to square one."

Sterling pointed at the hat near my feet. "It needs to be fed."

"Huh?" I glanced at Jade.

Her confused expression morphed into one of surprise. "A blood offering."

"Whose?" I asked.

Sterling Charles pointed at me. "Yours."

"Mine! Why?" I almost took a step back off the circle but steeled myself. The last time I'd done that, I'd gotten myself abducted and locked away in a ship dungeon. Not that I thought Sterling was a threat, but still… A girl didn't make that mistake twice.

"You're the connection," Sterling said as if that clarified things. Then he cast his gaze over the length of Ida May's body. A too-sexy-for-his-own-good smile claimed his lips. "When this is all over, I'll take you for a ride on my beast."

"You bet your sweet ass, you will," she replied. "But let's get this part out of the way right this second." She stepped into him, pressing her solid hand against his transparent body. And to my surprise, the area where she touched him seemed to turn solid.

He glanced down at her hand. "That's interesting."

"Not as interesting as what's beneath these clothes." She placed her other hand to his waist and slipped her fingers beneath the hem of his shirt. "Oh Lord. These abs." She closed her eyes and actually let out a tiny moan.

He chuckled. "I'm glad you approve."

Then she tilted her head and pressed her bright red lips to his. Sterling Charles didn't miss a beat. His arm looped around her waist, and with one swift motion, he tipped her backward. She held on, her hands clasped behind his neck, and she lifted one leg up in the air, just like one might see in the old black-and-white movies. After what seemed like forever, he finally righted her, leaving Ida May panting.

"Wow," Jade said, her hand covering her mouth. "That was… really something."

"I'll say." Ida May eyed him hungrily. "I hope that was just a taste of more to come."

"Count on it." He mimed tipping his invisible hat to first me and then Jade. In the next moment, he was gone again.

"What the heck just happened here?" I asked, my head spinning with the fact Sterling Charles had just shown up in the circle and then spontaneously made out with Ida May.

"Looks like we got help when we needed it." Jade stared pointedly at the hat. "He said you're the connection. Got that dagger handy?"

Of course I did. I was still holding it. I raised my arm, showing I had it. "And what? You want me to stab myself?"

"Well, I wouldn't put it that way." Jade gave me a patient smile. "Just a small cut on your hand so you can get a few drops on the hat."

I eyed the gleaming blade and grimaced. "But why *me?*"

She pursed her lips together and furrowed her brows. "I know this sounds crazy, but the only finding spell I know of that uses a blood offering is when a DNA match is needed."

"So you're saying that I'm somehow related to Bo?" That was crazy. Wasn't it? Not unless he was some third or fourth cousin removed. Because I didn't have any other family. My mother had been an only child, and so was I. And as far as I knew, my father's extended family lived out west.

"I don't know. Maybe? I'm just saying that's what it looks like from here." She spread her arms out wide, and the magic started to pulse again. "Willing to give it a try to see what happens?"

"Yeah, Pyper. Grow some balls and draw some blood, girl," Ida May added.

I gave Ida May a dirty look. No doubt if she had to slice her palm open, we'd never hear the end of it.

"Hey!" Ida May held up her hands and wrinkled her nose. "Don't do it if you don't want to. Can't say I blame you. Who knows where that blade has been. I mean who cares what happens to that kid? You just met him right? Even if you are related, it's not like you owe him anything. It's not like he provides comic relief for you every day in your café. I think you can take a pass on this one."

"Oh for the love of…" I opened my hand and in one swift motion sliced my palm. I winced from the sharp sting and gritted my teeth as I watched the trickle of blood well in my hand. When I glanced up, Ida May was standing in front of me with a smug smile on her face.

"That wasn't so hard, was it?" she asked.

SPIRITS, BEIGNETS, AND A BAYOU BIKER GANG

I rolled my eyes. "You're such a pain in my butt."

"You know you love me." She twirled around with her arms open, clearly enjoying her moment in the spotlight.

"Pyper," Jade said, pointing to the hat. "Ready?"

"As ready as I'll ever be." As ready as one could be when messing around with a blood spell. A tiny shudder of apprehension shook me. If this worked, did it really mean I was related to Bo? I pushed the thought out of my mind. It didn't matter one way or the other at the moment. Our main goal was to find him, make sure he was okay, and then find Mia. There was no time to dwell on my personal anxieties.

I crouched down, balled my hand into a loose fist, and positioned it over the hat.

One drop. Two. When the third one hit, a thin trickle of smoke rose from the hat, slowly at first, then quickly escalating until the circle was so full of smoke I could no longer see Ida May or Jade. My eyes started to burn and my lungs constricted, sending me into an uncontrollable coughing fit. I was two seconds from leaving the circle just to clear my lungs when the smoke dissipated.

I let out a horrified gasp. Because right there in the middle of the circle, his eyes wild and his muscles taught, stood Bo… pointing a handgun straight at me.

# Chapter 19

"WHOA!" I RAISED my hands in the air, my heart thundering against my rib cage. "No one wants to hurt you."

A muscle twitched in his neck as his eyes bored into mine. "What do you want?"

"Nothing." I shook my head. "We only wanted to make sure you're safe."

"I can feel your magic, you know. That goes for the witch behind me." He kept the gun trained steadily on me. "If either of you try to curse me, I'm pulling the trigger. No questions asked."

Holy hell. This wasn't the same Bo I'd hired to take Julius and me out on the bayou. Or rather it was, only now he was hostile, paranoid, and slightly unhinged. "No one is going to curse you," I said in as reassuring a tone as I could muster. "I swear it."

"Well, I will if he shoots you," Ida May said, stomping up to stand beside him. "What the hell is wrong with you, dude? That's no way to thank the people trying to save your ass."

Bo jerked and trained his weapon on Ida May.

She let out an impatient huff and pushed his arms out of the way so the gun was no longer in her face. "Please. I'm already dead. Your bullets aren't going to change anything."

"What?" He relaxed his combat stance, now holding the gun with only one hand while keeping it pointed down toward the ground. "You don't look like a ghost."

"You don't recognize me? I'm Ida May, and I hear I'm an Instagram star. How often do you see a ghost surfing on a gator?"

"That was you?" he asked, his entire demeanor relaxing. "Damn. Nice moves."

She beamed at him. "Thanks."

I cleared my throat. "I don't mean to interrupt this bonding moment, but I don't know how much time we have."

Bo instantly stiffened again, and it didn't escape my notice that his grip tightened around the gun.

I let out a sigh. "I promise you, no one here wants to hurt you."

"Then what do you want?" There was a paranoid accusation in his tone.

"To help if you're in danger. I saw those men abduct you earlier today. If you're being held against your will, we'll do everything in our power to get you out of there."

He glanced around at the circle, then down at his decidedly solid body. A slow smile claimed his lips while that wild look in his eyes all but disappeared. "It appears I'm right here."

"Unfortunately, no. You're not," Jade said.

He spun to face her.

"I'm sorry," she continued. "You're only here while the spell lasts or until it's broken. The moment you step out of the circle, it's over."

He muttered a curse under his breath.

"But if you can tell us where you are, we'll come get you," she said.

But Bo shook his head. "No. It's not safe."

Ida May let out a cackle. "Safe? These two aren't much for worrying about whether something is safe or not. They have some weird drive to actually save people at all costs. If I were you, I'd just give them the information they're asking for, because they're not going to give you a moment's peace until you do."

He gave her an odd look. "And saving people is a bad thing?"

She shrugged. "No. It just gets boring after a while, you know? I mean, wouldn't you rather be dirty dancing with some hottie at a club in New Orleans than dealing with this crap?"

"Dirty dancing? Seriously?" He gave her a you've-got-to-be-kidding-me look.

She raised her hands, palms up, and shook her head. "Kids today. Such idiots. If you're going to turn your nose up at the opportunity to put your hands all over a hot chick at a club, that's your problem."

He opened his mouth, then closed it as he seemed to consider her logic.

"Bo," I said, losing my patience. "Are you being held against your will?"

His head jerked up and he started to shake his head, then stopped. "I guess technically I am."

"What does that mean?"

His expression turned blank, and when he answered, his response felt measured and practiced as if he been fed a line over and over again. "If I want a roof over my head, I do what Emerson tells me to."

"Did he tell you to stay put?" My heart started to pound. Had he been spelled like Hale had? Had his free will been taken away too?

"Not in so many words. But he did send his boys to get me. If I leave now, there'll be hell to pay." He shoved his hands in his pockets and hung his head. "There's nothing you can really do."

"Wrong!" Ida May shouted and waved her arms. "This is your chance, kid. If you want to get away from that douche bucket permanently, these ladies are the ones to listen to."

"And go where?" he shouted back at her. "I'm not a ghost. I need a place to sleep. Food. Clothes. What are my choices? Even if I do leave, he'll come after me, just like he does with everyone else. No. It's better if I just deal with him. It's not that bad."

"You sure about that?" I asked him. "He tried to light Hale on fire today."

"Fire? Hale?" He ran a hand through his shaggy black hair. "No way. I don't believe it. I could see him messing with Brex or Paulie like that. But Hale is his business partner. There is no business without Hale."

"I was there," I said. "Hale's legs were burned. He needs serious medical attention, but I doubt he's going to get it. He and Moxie left town earlier tonight, and they aren't coming back."

"Is that why Emerson hasn't come to the compound yet?" he asked, his eyes wide and full of fear.

"No. He's been apprehended by the Witches' Council, and

with any luck, he's being incarcerated right now while he waits to stand trial. I'd really like to get you out of the snake pit before the rest of the club finds out about it."

His shoulders slumped. "Then what? Just go on with life like normal? Keep working at the Mayhem Tours company? Keep sleeping on a cot in Emerson's shitty rental house, until the power is shut off, while he lives in his mini mansion across town?"

"It doesn't have to be that way. We want to help you find a permanent solution. One that lets you concentrate on your future instead of condemning you to a life of crime."

"I'm not a criminal," he said, indignation clear in his tone. "I don't have anything to do with any of that. I'm a tour guide. That's it."

"I believe you," I said softly. "But what do you think is going to happen to you if you stay here? If for some reason Emerson manages to squirm his way out of this current problem, what do you think he's going to be make you do next? Right now you're an extra paycheck from the government. Once you turn eighteen, what will he do then? Surely he won't let you live in his house out of the goodness of his heart. There'll be payments to be made, and if I had to guess, they'd come in the form of favors. Ones that could land you in prison."

He scowled and started to pace. After a minute, he grabbed his hair with both hands and let out a loud scream of frustration.

I met Jade's gaze from across the circle. The helpless look on her face mirrored what I felt in my gut.

"That's it. Let it out," Ida May said and patted his back.

"We all need to make a little noise every now and then."

He stepped away, rejecting her touch, but it didn't seem to faze her. She just crossed her arms over her chest, looked him up and down, and asked, "Done yet?"

"For now," he ground out.

"Good. Now man up and tell Pyper where you're being held so she and wonder witch over there can go save your ass."

He started to shake his head and opened his mouth to speak, but she held up a hand, cutting him off.

"Nope. Don't even go there. The strongest thing a man can do is to admit when he needs a little help. So unless you think you can just walk out of that place, jump in your truck, and drive right out of this one-gator town, you best start talkin'."

He stared at her, his mouth still open. Then he gave her just a hint of a smile. "One-gator town?"

"I didn't see any horses hanging around, now did I?"

"No, Miss Ida May, you probably didn't." There was still a trace of humor in his tone when he turned to me and said, "There's no official address. It's on the south end of Bayou Charles off Black Sands Road. Look for the polka-dot panties."

"Panties?" I echoed.

He nodded. "Hanging from a faded sign. After you pass the sign, go another five hundred feet and turn onto the dirt road. There's only one way in and one way out. Expect to encounter at least a dozen bikers. I'll be in the back, cooking in the kitchen." Resentment clouded his deep blue eyes.

"We'll be there as soon as we can," I promised.

"If you say so," he said.

"We say so," Jade added. "Just be ready to hightail it out of there at a moment's notice. All right? No running back in for your phone or cash or anything else."

"Fine. Ain't nothing I need here anyway." He glanced around curiously and then frowned, that muscle once again pulsing in his neck. "The spell is fading. I'm being pulled back into the—"

He disappeared with a small pop.

The three of us stood there, staring at each other for a moment. Then Jade shrugged. "Better figure out how we're going to get there. The three of us aren't going to fit on the motorcycle.

I eyed Ida May. She was grinning and rubbing her hands together as if it were Christmas morning at Jade's implication that she'd be invited. Sighing, I nodded. Besides, if we took the bike there'd be no room for Bo. "I think I know someone who can help out."

# Chapter 20

"DID SOMEONE SAY they needed a ride?" Miss Kitty asked as she glided into the entry of the inn wearing a bright red, white, and blue maxi dress with a gold Wonder Woman–style cinch belt. But the outfit wouldn't have been complete without her gold wristbands and gold lamé knee-high boots.

"Damn, Kitty. You look hot!" Ida May strode over to the older woman. "Where did you get those boots?"

"At a secondhand place in Thibodaux. Can you believe someone gave these up? I'm going to wear these like a boss."

"You already are," I said. The boots were pretty fabulous. But the entire outfit was a little on the loud side. Just like Miss Kitty. Trying to be stealthy was going to be a challenge. Between her and Ida May, one of them was bound to blow our cover.

"Let's get a move on. I have a live chat scheduled first thing in the morning. My fans can't get enough of that ghost video."

"You mean I'm famous?" Ida May fluffed her curly hair and plastered a smug smile on her lips. "I always knew I was destined to be a star."

"You…" Miss Kitty paused to really study Ida May. "Omigod!" She pulled out her phone and tapped the screen.

She stared at it, then held the phone up beside Ida May, comparing the ghost on the video to the one on her screen. She let out a squeal of delight. "You're a ghost! I just met a real live ghost." She tapped a few more buttons on the phone and then paused again. "I'm about to go live on Facebook. Is that okay? I want to share this experience with my followers."

Ida May shrugged. "Why not?"

"Uh, Miss Kitty?" I cut in, frustrated at the derailing. "Now isn't really the best time for this. Maybe after we get Bo, the two of you can discuss live streaming or group chat or whatever you need to do?"

"Right. Right. Sorry." She waved a hand. "I let myself get carried away. Let's go get that young man."

Ida May slipped her arm though Miss Kitty's. "I like you. If I'd lived to see my golden years, I think I'd have been just like you. Feisty is my favorite trait."

"Oh honey. You're so kind to say that. Now tell me, how did you end up a ghost and how is it you're here with us now?" Miss Kitty poked at Ida May's bare arm. "I mean, if I hadn't seen you on my video, I'd have never known you're not… you know, alive. Or are you? Are you a witch with the ability to tame gators and make yourself invisible?"

Ida May's high laugh rang through the inn. "That's a long story. I'll fill you in later."

I sucked in a deep breath, and with Jade just behind me, we followed them out the door.

When we got to the CRV, Miss Kitty tossed the keys at me. "You drive. I'm too wound up. Imagine… a real live ghost."

"What happened to your monster truck?" I asked, curious.

She shrugged. "Not enough seats. Not unless someone

wanted to ride in the back."

"No thanks. This is perfect." I climbed into the front seat, Jade the front passenger seat, while the two jokesters giggled their way into the back. I glanced over at Jade. "Does Black Sands Road show up on Google Maps?"

"Yep." She flashed her phone toward me. "Nothing about polka-dot panties though."

"They need to up their game."

✧　✧　✧

"What's that?" Jade leaned forward, peering through the window.

"I don't see anything except creepy tree shadows," I said.

"You should turn the brights on," Miss Kitty said. "You wouldn't believe how many people run right off the road right into the bayou for being careless. And I didn't live for seven decades just to become gator food."

"Don't worry, Miss Kitty," Ida May said. "I'm the alligator whisperer, remember? I'll protect you."

"Sure. But what about my boots? They won't survive bayou mud."

"True." Ida May leaned forward between the seats. "Make sure you don't dump us in the water. The trauma from boot-death would be too much to bear."

"For the love of…"

"That's it. Right there. The billboard Bo was talking about." Jade pointed straight ahead.

I slowed and pulled to the side to let the lights—already in bright mode—illuminate the faded signage. It read: Get Trashed at Jerry's Junkyard and Tavern. "Classy."

Jade started to giggle, and it took me a moment to figure out what was so funny. A grizzled man wearing overalls was holding a handle of some sort, but it was positioned right at his crotch, making it appear to be something else entirely. "Is that a shovel?"

"I don't know what it is exactly, but I know what it looks like."

"Those polka-dot panties are hanging off his woody," Miss Kitty said. "I hope that's a caricature and not representative of his actual size. Because damn, wouldn't that be a disappointment?"

"You haven't seen small until you've seen a micro-penis." Ida May held her thumb and index finger together. "I mean, we're talking maybe an inch."

"No! How did that work?" In the review mirror, I noted Miss Kitty had turned to face Ida May. She had a strange mix of amusement and horror in her expression.

Ida May laughed. "Let's just say he was good with his—"

"Stop!" I waved my hands in the air. "Now is not the time for slumber party gossip."

"Really?" Ida May waved a hand at the sign. "How can anyone look at Billy Bob Boner up there, with those panties hanging off the end of his... ah, handle... and decide it isn't time for a little girl talk?"

"That is not a boner—Never mind." I pulled back onto the road. "Just keep a lookout for the dirt road."

The two in the back ignored me, continuing their conversation on size preference. "What did I do to deserve this?" I asked Jade.

She gave me a wan smile. "You wouldn't have it any other

way."

"Really?" I snorted and inched along. "I think I could live without the instructions on how to work with a micro-penis."

She snickered. "At least they're entertaining. And you deserve them because they amuse you."

"If you say so."

"Here it is. To the right," Jade said.

I pulled to the side of the road and took a deep breath. "Ready for this?"

"No, but we don't have a choice, do we?"

We did, but we'd do what we felt we had to, even if it meant walking into a situation we had no way of analyzing. We could've literally been walking into a trap.

Jade closed her eyes and cocked her head to the side, concentrating. Grimacing, she said, "We can't just drive up to the house. There are too many of them, and they're already amped up. Probably wondering what's keeping Emerson."

"So what do you think?" I asked her. "Park the car on the road and walk up?"

"No way," Miss Kitty interjected, her tone all business. "Switch places with me and Ida May. I'll drive up, and before we get to the house we can drop you off. Ida May and I will distract those boys while you get that nice kid out of there."

"I don't think—" I started.

"That's the perfect plan." Ida May already had her door open. "If anyone knows how to fluster men, it's me. And they won't dare mess with Miss Kitty. Between those boots and her sass, they'll be lining up for her attention."

"That's right." Miss Kitty puffed up with the praise.

"I mean, who doesn't want a cool surrogate mamaw?" Ida

May said with a flourish.

"Hey!" Miss Kitty scowled at her.

"What?" Ida May asked.

"Don't go underestimating me. I still have plenty of game. How do you think I snagged Hot Handyman?"

"Hot Handyman?" Ida May asked, sudden interest in her gaze. "I'm going to need a cocktail for this story, aren't I?"

Miss Kitty gave her a devilish smile. "More like two."

"This could go on all night," Jade said to me. "I think Miss Kitty's plan is a decent one. None of those men are going to mess with her, and if they do, Ida May is there to knock them upside the head. In the meantime, we can get Bo out of there before anyone notices."

"You're right. That could work." I gripped the steering wheel until my knuckles turned white. I wasn't worried about Ida May. She could hold her own. But Miss Kitty... I'd never forgive myself if anything happened to her.

My door opened, and before I could react, Miss Kitty reached in and grabbed my arm. "Out! I'm driving now."

I was jerked out of the driver's seat and nearly landed on my butt before I steadied myself by grabbing the door. "Okay, okay! You can drive. Just at the first sign of any magic or if anyone even looks at you wrong, get the hell out of there. Got it?"

Miss Kitty saluted me. "Got it, captain."

Jade and I switched places with Miss Kitty and Ida May. Miss Kitty took command of the wheel and slowly maneuvered down the narrow dirt road. For once, neither one said anything, opting instead to pay close attention to the road and their surroundings.

Miss Kitty stopped the car abruptly. "Get out here."

I peered over her shoulder and frowned. "Why? It looks like we're a ways from the house."

"No we're not." She pointed to the left. "See the light?"

I squinted and finally spotted it through the dense vegetation. "I do now. Good catch."

"The house must be just around the bend," she added. "Meet me back here in ten minutes."

"Will do." With a nod to Jade, we both hopped out of the car, careful not to slam our doors. We stepped back out of the way, covered our mouths, and waited as the car kicked up a cloud of dust.

"Let's go," Jade said, breaking into a jog. "I can't wait to see what kind of trouble those two cause."

Jade and I kept close the tree line, staying well away from the lights of the vehicle. And when we got to the clearing, I paused.

Miss Kitty had backed the car in so it was facing the dirt road we'd just come in on. Smart. That would make for an easier getaway. And the pair we already walking up to the large cabin.

The place was a wood-sided, two-story cottage that looked as if it'd been slapped together with tree sap and duct tape. The sagging front porch was illuminated by one hanging lightbulb. The screen on the door had been ripped in multiple places, rendering it utterly useless. Tin foil covered the old windows, and the wood siding was rotted in multiple places. The place could be a meth lab for all we knew.

Ida May and Miss Kitty hopped out of the vehicle. They met up for a second, then sauntered up the front steps. Ida May paused at the door, adjusted her, ahem, assets, smoothed her hair, and then with a nod from Miss Kitty, she knocked on the door and yelled, "Jerry! Open up. I need a drink five minutes ago!"

The door swung open as if the big, bald-headed biker standing inside the cabin had been waiting. "There's no Jerry here," he ground out and started to close the door.

"Wait!" Ida May said. "Isn't this Jerry's Junkyard and Tavern? We saw a sign on the main road."

"Jerry's what?" He gave her a look that clearly said he thought she was crazy.

"Tavern. Bar. Place to get trashed and pick up a burly biker guy for the evening." Ida May made a point of exaggerating her movements as she looked him up and down. Someone like… you, actually. Is any of this ringing a bell?"

"Looks like we have the wrong establishment," Miss Kitty said, tugging on Ida May's arm. "Sorry, young man. We didn't mean to bother anyone. We'll just be going."

"Oh hell." Ida May pouted. "You sure there's no party going on in there?" she asked the biker. "With that sign back there and all these motorcycles, we thought for sure we'd come to the right place. You have no idea how much the rumble of a custom motor really gets my engine going."

Another biker appeared next to the bald-headed one. He had long, dark, unkempt hair and some sort of tattoo covering his neck and half his left cheek. "Ladies!" He held his hands out wide. "Welcome. Don't mind Fisk. He sometimes forgets his manners. Come on in. Of course you found the party. What can I get you to drink? Beer or whiskey? Or both?"

"Both," Ida May and Miss Kitty said at the same time.

"Of course they want both," I muttered as the two

disappeared inside. "Can you imagine those two intoxicated?"

"Actually, yes," Jade whispered in an amused tone. "But hopefully we won't be here long enough to witness that tonight. Come on."

The pair of us ran across the dusty property hunched over. There wasn't a lot to have to try to hide from. The tin foil on the windows meant that while we couldn't see in, they also couldn't see out. But that didn't mean there weren't cameras set up around the property. In fact, there probably were. We were in luck though, because the moon was hidden and except for the ambient light from the porch, most of the property was bathed in shadows.

We skirted around to the back and immediately flattened ourselves against the cabin when we spotted three bikers standing around a garbage-can fire. Thankfully there was a radio playing somewhere and the sound from our movement must've been muffled because none of them turned to look in our direction.

"Now what?" I whispered to Jade.

She glanced at the back door and then over to the bikers. Biting her lower lip, she wrinkled her nose. "We need a distraction."

"Short of yelling fire, I don't know what that would be." My palms started to sweat, and I reached for my dagger just to calm myself.

"I've got an idea, but I want you to make your way to the back door first."

I hesitated. "I don't think it's a good idea to separate."

"I'll be right behind you." Magic was already glowing in her palms.

"All right. But be careful."

"Aren't I always?" She smiled innocently.

"Right. Just like I am." With a roll of my eyes, I darted over to the back of the cabin and gingerly made my way up the stairs, praying they weren't so rotted that I fell straight through. On the top step, the porch groaned and I froze.

"Hey, Bobo, is that you? Bring us more beers," one of the bikers called.

I held my breath and ducked behind a wooden picnic table. A moment later, I heard the rumble of thunder followed by a bolt of lightning that hit one of the nearby trees. A loud crack preceded the even louder thump of one of the limbs crashing to the ground.

"Jesus! Where the hell did that come from," one of the bikers yelled as the three of them cowered and glanced around for any more falling debris.

"It wasn't supposed to storm until tomorrow," another said.

"It isn't storming, you jackass," the third one added as he stared up into the inky sky.

"What do you think thunder and lightning is? Nature's music?"

The three of them continued to bicker while Jade crept up onto the porch. "Hopefully that keeps them distracted for a few minutes." She glanced down at my knife. "You might want to put that away. It's glowing."

"It is?" Holy hell, she was right. Blue light danced over the blade, and I realized I'd inadvertently called on my own magic. My defenses had snapped into place, preparing me for battle. Well, better ready than caught with my pants down so to speak. "Sorry." I shoved it back into the sheath at my belt but kept my hand on the hilt, just in case.

"Ready?" she asked.

I nodded. "Ready."

She reached for the door handle, paused, and said, "There's an energy block on the place. I can't tell how many people are in there."

"We're just going to have to trust that Ida May and Miss Kitty are keeping everyone entertained." If anyone could, it was them.

"All right." Jade took a deep breath and opened the back door. No light spilled out of what appeared to be a mudroom.

We crept past beat-up old riding boots and musty, dirty towels piled up in the corner. Light shone under a dilapidated door. I pressed my ear to it and heard high-pitched and lower-register deep rumblings coming from somewhere within the house. "Looks like now is a good time."

"I'll go. You keep watch." She already had her hand on the knob when I stopped her.

"But you don't even know what he looks like."

"You think there's more than one seventeen-year-old hanging out in the kitchen?"

"Good point."

She gave me a reassuring smile and then opened the door and walked in like she had every right to be there. I stayed pressed up against the rough wall, waiting.

"Bo?" I heard Jade ask, her tone light and reassuring.

"Who are you?" he asked, suspicious.

"Pyper's friend. I was there when we brought you to the circle earlier. You ready to get out of here?"

"Where is she? And what exactly do those two think they're

doing out there? They're acting like idiots and are going to get themselves hurt if the guys find out they're part of this."

"Pyper's keeping watch. And those two are distracting everyone. Don't worry about them. They can take care of themselves."

Damn, I hoped that was true. I was worried. Ida May could probably talk herself out of anything, and even if she didn't, what were they going to do to her that was worse than death? But what about Miss Kitty?

"The longer we stand around in this kitchen, the more likely someone's going to notice," Jade said.

"Are you the witch?"

"Yes."

There was a long pause, then he said, "All right. Let's go."

Footsteps shuffled across what must have been old wood floors. And a moment later, Bo appeared in the mudroom. I smiled at him and wrapped my hand around his arm, squeezing in reassurance.

"Let's hurry," Jade said as she followed him. I turned and reached for the back door.

"I don't think so," a gruff voice said.

Jade sucked in a sharp breath.

I spun back around and froze.

A big, burly man with short gray hair and a salt-and-pepper beard stood to the side of her, his 9mm Glock pointed right at her head.

# Chapter 21

"WHO ARE YOUR friends, Bo?" The man's conversational tone sent a chill up my spine.

Bo stiffened beside me, then slipped his arm over my shoulder, tucking me into his side. "Just some chicks I met the other day. They came to party like the other two did. Got a problem with that?"

"No, no problem." But he didn't lower the gun, and he was eyeing me with suspicion. "If they're here to party, where are you headed?"

"Outside. Jesus, Dutch, what's with the third degree?" Bo dropped his arm and stepped forward, putting his body between Dutch's and mine.

Jade stood still, her eyes darting from Bo to Dutch. Magic didn't spark in her palms. What was that about? She should've been able to knock him out without even really trying.

"Emerson ordered me to keep an eye on you until he got here. And that is what I'm going to do." Dutch jerked his head toward the interior of the house. "Now get your ass back in the living room or I'm about to turn these two bitches into a life lesson for you."

"Did you just call us bitches?" I blurted out and darted

around Bo. With hands on my hips, I stared up at him, waiting for his response. And though I couldn't care less what he called us, I needed to get closer to him if I wanted to help Jade. She was one powerful witch, and the only reason she'd be standing there letting someone put a gun to her head was if for some reason her powers were neutralized. Lucky for her, mine weren't.

"I'll call you any damned thing I want to. Now get your ass inside or you're going to watch your witch friend die right before your eyes." He reached out and grabbed my arm, yanking me forward… and giving me the perfect opening.

Power surged up from the depths of my soul. My hand wrapped around the hilt of my dagger, and as I fell into him, I didn't hesitate. With one swing, I buried the knife in his left shoulder.

The big biker went down in a heap, and the gun skittered across the torn-up linoleum.

"Are you okay?" I asked Jade.

Her face had gone white, and she was shaking.

"What's wrong?"

She knelt down and picked up a tiny dart. Holding her hand out, she said, "That bastard pricked me with this. I think it's meant to knock someone out, but because I'm a witch, it only succeeded in momentarily neutralizing my powers." Blowing out a breath, she held her hand up, demonstrating a faint spark of magic. "It's already returning though. An herbal pill will have me back to my old self in no time. We have to get out of here. Now."

"What a total creep," I said, terrified of what went down in this house on a regular basis.

Bo grimaced, reached down, and picked up the gun. Then he stared down at the lifeless body of Dutch. "Did you kill him?"

I shook my head. "No. He's just incapacitated for the moment."

"Here." Jade stood over him, her hands out, and with what appeared to be great effort, she wove thin ropes of magic around his wrists and ankles. "He isn't going anywhere for now. Grab your knife and let's go."

I did as she said, sent Miss Kitty a quick text to get out of there, and then the three of us hurried out the back door.

"Hey, Bo! Is that you?" one of the fire pit guys asked.

"Yeah. Why?" Bo answered.

"What are you doing?" I hissed.

"Making sure they stay where they are," he muttered.

"Bring me another six pack, will ya?"

"Sure," he called back but didn't stop following Jade. "It'll be just a few. I'm running an errand for Dutch."

"Hurry, will ya? I'm almost dry."

Jesus. Did they make Bo do everything? What was he, the male version of Cinderella?

"I'm on it," Bo called back. Then he leaned toward me. "We'd better be out of here before they get antsy."

"Oh, we will be." As soon as we rounded the house, the three of us took off down the dirt road. Within moments we heard the front door open and loud voices carry out of the house.

"Sorry, boys! The old man is on a rampage," I heard Miss Kitty say. "If I'm not home in twenty, he's threatening to cut up my lingerie. I can't have that. You know how much I spend at

Victoria's Secret every month? It's a small fortune. Not to mention the lace G-strings and crotchless panties. I mean, that stuff doesn't just grow on trees."

"Crotchless?" One of the guys roared with laughter. "You go, grandma."

"You're a sweetie," she said.

"And you're raunchy. I mean, why wear any at all if it's crotchless?" Ida May asked. "If access is what you're after, you can't beat commando."

"I like her," one of the guys said.

"And I want to do her!" another called. That comment was met with catcalls and wolf whistles.

"Well, aren't you a charmer?" Ida May said on a high laugh. "Maybe next time."

"Like tomorrow?" he asked hopefully.

But no one answered, and the next thing I knew, the CRV was rolling down the lane toward us. Miss Kitty pulled to a stop, rolled down her window, and said, "Need a lift?"

I grinned at her and Ida May. "Well played, ladies."

"Looks like we got what we came for," Ida May said, peering at Bo. "Get in so I can shower when we get back to the inn. I've never felt so dirty in my life."

I raised my eyebrows in disbelief. "Seriously?"

"Seriously. Just because I worked in Storyville doesn't mean I didn't have standards. There was one in there who was picking his scabs and eating them. Another kept scratching his balls... inside his pants. Can you imagine what he was harboring in there?" She shuddered. "Disgusting."

My skin started to crawl. "Gross."

"You're telling me." She wrapped her arms around herself

and shook her head as if to erase the memories.

I waited as Jade and Bo climbed in the backseat. And just when I lifted my foot to follow, a loud shot rang through the night, shattering the back window.

I dove in, yelling, "Go! Go! Go!"

The car fishtailed down the dirt road as more bullets peppered the back and whizzed by us. Miss Kitty stepped on the gas and never slowed down once, not even to turn onto the main road.

"Holy hell," I said, my heart hammering so hard I thought it'd burst right out of my chest.

"Is everyone all right back there?" Miss Kitty called over her shoulder.

"I think so," Jade said.

"Bo?" Miss Kitty asked.

"Yeah," he said, lifting his head from his ducked position.

"I'm fine," I added. "Ida May? How about you?"

"I'm not hit, but…" She turned around, giving us a good look at her head and torso. Her flesh was disappearing rapidly, making her look diseased as she turned back into her ghostly form.

"Oh, Ida May." I reached out to grab her hand, but as soon as I did, her flesh turned to sand and disappeared into the ether.

"Whoa. That's… creepy," Bo said.

"That's rude," Ida May said, scowling at him. "Would you want someone telling you you're creepy after your dead?"

"Umm… I'd be dead right?"

"Well, yes. That's the idea," she snapped.

"I guess if I'm dead and talking to someone, they have every right to think I'm creepy."

"You didn't think I was creepy when I was helping save your butt," she countered. "You guys are all the same. As long as there are fleshy boobs in your face, you're happy. The minute a girl morphs back into her true form, you run away like scared little toddlers. I don't get it."

"Come on, Ida May," Miss Kitty said, laughing. "That's not really fair. Pretty much anytime guys stop staring at the boobs, they start to run. It's not unique to ghosts. Trust me on that one."

Ida May flipped back around and crossed her arms over her chest. The movement made the rest of her flesh flake away, leaving her 100 percent in ghost form.

*I guess Pyper's the only one who can see me now?* she asked.

When no one answered, she let out an exaggerated sigh. *It was nice while it lasted.*

"Is she gone?" Bo asked.

"Nope. Just silenced," I said. "But don't worry. She's fine."

*That's what you think,* Ida May said and then disappeared from the car.

✧    ✧    ✧

"I CAN'T BELIEVE you drove that far with no lights on," I said to Miss Kitty as we exited the inn's garage. We'd decided to hide her car in there for the time being. It was too easy to identify now with all the bullet holes in the back.

"It's just one of my many talents." Her words were flippant, but her body language was not. Dark circles lined her eyes and she wobbled slightly as she walked.

"Here, Miss Kitty." Bo held his arm out to the older woman. "Let me walk you in."

"I'm fine." She brushed him aside and sped up, but the heel on her gold boot slipped off the paver and she started to crumple.

"Whoa, Miss Kitty!" Bo caught her just before she went down and propped her back up on her feet. "I gotcha."

"Oh my," she said, breathless. "I almost went ass over teakettle."

Bo chuckled. "Almost." He wrapped his arm around her waist and guided her through the back door.

"He's a sweet kid," Jade said to me.

I nodded.

"Are you going to tell him?"

"Tell him what? That his guardian is a piece of crap? I think he already knows that."

She tilted her head to the side and gave me an impatient look. "No. That you two are related."

"We don't know that for sure," I said, hedging.

"We know. The blood wouldn't have worked if you weren't. It's the same spell I used when I summoned my father… my real father… last year." She placed her hand on my arm. "I know you don't have any family except for Kane—"

"And you," I said, trying to ignore the sharp stab of pain in my heart. I'd thought I'd made peace with the fact I was on my own. But learning Bo might be my relative… It was too much. Fear warred with my deep-seated desire for that thing everyone else had but I didn't—family.

"And me." Jade smiled. "There's never any changing that now. But Pyper, you have to know. If you let this go, you'll always regret it."

I knew she was right. I just wasn't ready. "We need to find

Mia first. Then we can figure out the rest."

"Whatever you say." She tied her thick strawberry-blond hair up into a bun, a sign she was ready to get down to business. "Let's get to work. We still have a girl to rescue."

We found Miss Kitty and Bo sitting at the small breakfast table in the kitchen. I headed straight for the coffeemaker and started brewing a large pot. It was well past midnight, but I wasn't going to make it without several shots of caffeine.

"Do you have any food in this place?" Bo asked.

"Whatever Moxie left in the fridge." I waved a hand, indicating he should help himself. As I pulled out mugs for the coffee, he scavenged the kitchen. Coffee cake, blueberry muffins, blackberry cobbler, and vanilla ice cream all made it to the table.

Jade found plates and utensils, and by the time I poured the coffee, they were all digging in to their indulgence of choice.

I took a slice of coffee cake but barely nibbled as I studied Bo. That vague sense of familiarity hit me again, but I wasn't sure why. I studied his face, his angular jawline, the raven, wavy hair, brilliant blue eyes. Besides our eyes and hair color, we really didn't look alike, at least not that I could tell. He was almost a foot taller than I was, different nose and chin. But those eyes. They were the same ones I'd been staring at my entire life.

Bo looked up from his cobbler and met my gaze. "You're creeping me out."

My lips twitched as I took a sip of coffee.

He shoveled in a few more bites, then put his fork down. "Are you going to tell me who you are?"

"Excuse me?"

"People don't just go out of their way to help people they just met. So you either want something from me or you're some kind of saint. Which is it?"

"My money's on both," Miss Kitty said, her eyes sparkling.

Jade laughed and covered Miss Kitty's hand. "I hate to disappoint you, but she's no saint."

"Hey!" I cast her a mock offended look.

"Then you want something from me." Bo propped his elbows on the table. "What is it?"

I sighed and put my coffee mug down. "Information, if you have it."

Wariness clouded his eyes and the interest vanished. "Emerson doesn't tell me anything."

"It's not about him," I said. "Though I'm certain the council will want to talk to you at some point."

He sat back in his chair, slumping one shoulder while he watched me with suspicion.

Damn. That wasn't the attitude I was looking for. "Let me start at the beginning." I launched into the explanation of meeting Sterling Charles, the information on Mia and the clue about the "key."

Bo sucked in a sharp breath. "You're saying this ghost says Mia is still alive?" His voice cracked when he said Mia's name.

"Yes. And I believe you might literally be the key to finding her."

His face turned ashen as he stared at me. Then as if someone had flipped a switch, he sat straight up and brought his fist down on the table with a roar of frustration.

I jumped, startled by his outburst, but Jade and Miss Kitty just sat there, totally unfazed.

"You're a sick person," Bo ground out. "How dare you come here, pretend to give a shit about my life, and then lay this crap on me."

"I—"

"Mia died a long time ago. Whatever you thought you heard, it was wrong." He stood up so fast the chair fell backward, clattering to the floor. He gave me one last look of disgust before he strode out of the room.

That sharp pain in my chest intensified. The urge to get up and follow him was so overwhelming I was already rising before I even gave it conscious thought.

"Mia is alive?" Miss Kitty covered her mouth as tears welled in her eyes.

"We have reason to believe she is," I said, wondering if that was even true. I only had the word of one ghost. They weren't always reliable, and yet I'd bought his story hook, line, and sinker. Just because her body had never been found didn't mean she hadn't been fed to the gators We were in the bayou after all.

"You should be totally honest with him," Jade said quietly. "He needs someone he can trust."

"That's not going to happen overnight." A sick feeling took up residence in my gut. The reality of Bo having no one in his life he could count on was too much.

"You have to start somewhere," Jade said.

"You're right." I poured two more cups of coffee and went off in search of the one person I might be able to call family.

# Chapter 22

"HEY," I SAID to Bo and set both mugs down on the coffee table in the living room. A faint trace of Moxie's lavender perfume lingered, making me wonder if we'd ever see them again. "Mind if I join you?"

He crossed his arms over his chest and shrugged one shoulder. "It's not my house."

"It's not mine either. But you can tell me to go away if you don't want to talk to me." I smiled gently. "I'll go if you want me to, and I'll even leave the coffee."

He glanced over at the table. "Cream and sugar?"

"Yes to both."

Inching forward, he grabbed one of the mugs. "Thanks."

"You're welcome." I waved at the other end of the couch. "Is this okay?"

He nodded and sat back into the cushions.

"There's something I need to tell you," I blurted and then mentally cringed. That wasn't exactly how I'd imagined broaching the subject.

"You have some other ulterior motive for blowing up my life with Emerson?"

"No. I admit that it appears I want something from you,

but it's only information. Getting you out of that house was just the right thing to do. Emerson is a dangerous man, and—"

"You don't think I know he's dangerous? I'm the one who's had to live with him for four years. But what choice did I have? My father dumped me off on him, and without Emerson, I'd be a homeless street bum. So say what you want, but at least there was food in the fridge and a place for me to sleep."

"You need more than just blankets and burgers," I said.

"It turns out that's not entirely accurate." The steel in his tone and expression scared me. He was entirely too young to be so hardened.

"I hear you, but maybe we can change that."

"What's that mean? Gonna call social services and get me a new family? Because if that's the case, I should start walking back to Emerson's. When he's released, he'll just find me anyway."

He was probably right. If he knew anything about Emerson's business, the biker would never let him leave in peace. But not if I had anything to say about it. "You know that spell we did earlier that landed you in the magical circle?"

"Yeah." He stared down into his coffee mug but made no movement to take a drink.

"Well, there's something interesting that happened. We were using the hat you lost at Mayhem Gator Tours. You know, when those other bikers forced you into the SUV?"

"You have my hat?" He glanced around the room as if it would magically appear.

"We have your hat, but it, uh... well, probably needs a cleaning."

"It needed one before I lost it. It'll be fine."

"It has blood on it." Before he had a chance to process that statement, I plowed on, explaining the blood sacrifice and that Jade was certain we were related in some way.

"Related?" He frowned. "That's not possible." Shaking his head, he added, "I know your eyes are the same as mine, but there's nothing else. Besides, my mother was an only child and only had two kids. And my father." He snorted. "All his family is out west somewhere. Arizona, Utah. Maybe even California. You're not from there, are you?"

I shook my head. "No. And my mother only had one sister, but she died at a young age."

We sat there silently, contemplating what I was suggesting.

Finally Bo spoke up. "What's your last name?"

"Rayne. Yours?"

"Bowman."

"Bowman," I breathed as my insides turned to jelly. "Your father's name?"

"Red." He watched me curiously. "Are we cousins or something?"

The backs of my eyes stung, and I did nothing to stop the tears from silently rolling down my face as I shook my head. "No, definitely not cousins."

He put his coffee mug down on the table, picked up a tissue box, and handed it to me. "Then why are you crying? Are you that relieved you're not related to a loser like me?" His tone was light, but something in his eyes told me that's exactly the way he saw himself.

"Not a loser, and we are related." I stood and crossed the room, grabbing the leather handbag I'd left there earlier in the evening. After rummaging around, I eventually put my fingers on the item I'd been looking for. I held up the photograph and asked, "Recognize this man? He's my father."

He took the old, beat-up photo from me, squinted, then threw it down on the table. "So. You're my half-sister then. Did good old Dad come back to you after he decided I wasn't worth the effort?"

"Back to me? Hardly. I haven't seen that man since I was five years old. And I have no desire to do so now. But you..." The tears started to flow again.

Bo started to look panicky at the idea of dealing with a blubbering idiot.

"Hold on," I said, forcing a smile. "Let me just splash some water on my face." I disappeared into the nearest restroom and stared at my blank expression in the mirror. It was as if I'd had too much brain stimulation and could no longer continue to function. Squaring my shoulders, I strode back into the room, determined to keep my emotions in check.

Bo sat on the edge of the couch, studying the photo. I stood there waiting until he finally looked up. "How old were you when this picture was taken?"

"I don't know. Four? Five maybe? He left shortly after that. I never heard from him again."

Bo blew out a breath. "Five years old." Closing his eyes, he shook his head. "He left me when I was twelve. I guess I don't have much to complain about compared to what you must've gone through."

"I don't think it's something that can be compared. Pain is pain no matter what the circumstances are."

He picked up an abandoned pen, popped the top button with his thumb, snapped it again, and continued the motion, filling the room with a constant click, click, click sound. It was hypnotic in a way, something to focus on while we both processed this new reality. Finally he paused. "He only stayed as long as he did because my mother died."

The words hit me like a sucker punch. Not only had our bastard father left him with Emerson Charles, but he'd done it after the kid had lost his mom. And for what? "Do you have any idea where he went?"

"None." Bo's expression turned cold. "He told me one day it was time for him to move on. That I was man enough to take care of myself, and that was that. He packed his bags, dropped me off with Emerson, and took off, never looking back."

"Son of a... That bastard," I said almost to myself.

"Yeah. But you know what? I don't need him. I don't need anybody." His muscles were taut with tension and his tone full of conviction.

I recognized something in him I'd long harbored within myself. A fierce determination to survive, to make something of myself if only to prove that I could. "Everyone needs someone, Bo."

He barked out a humorless laugh. "People only disappoint you in the end."

My heart hurt. He was only seventeen. I ached to wrap my arms around him and make promises of a better future. But I couldn't. Not yet. Trust would be hard earned from a boy who'd lived a life of heartbreak. Instead, I said, "I'd really like a chance to prove I'm not one of those people."

He cast me a sideways glance. "What, just because we share DNA, you think you owe me something? Well, forget it. I don't need you or your charity."

"Bo, I didn't know until about a half hour ago that we're related. The minute I saw you forced into that SUV, I was planning how to find you."

"Right, because you think I know something about my sister's disappearance."

"Oh hell." I stood up, suddenly unable to stay seated. How had I forgotten that? Did that mean I'd just gained a sister too? "Do you mean *our* sister?"

"No." He got up and started to pace the edge of the area rug. "*My* sister. Not yours. She and I have different fathers. But if you think for one minute that I knew something about her disappearance and never said anything to anyone, then you're as crazysauce as the rest of them. Mia was the only person who had ever been there for me. The *only* one, got it? And I'd do anything to help her."

I let the words hang in the air for a moment. Then I stared him straight in the eye and said, "If that's true, then here's your chance. I believe there is a decent possibility that she's still alive, and that unbeknownst to you, you might be the answer to finding her."

He threw his hands up. "What am I supposed to do with that? I can't provide information I'm not aware I have."

Jade appeared under the arch and cleared her throat.

When we both turned to look at her, she walked into the room, straight up to Bo, and took his hands in hers. Staring him in the eye, she asked, "Do you want to find your sister?"

His eyes closed and a visible tremor shook his body as he nodded.

"Then I can help. With you here, all we need to do now is perform a finding spell."

I sucked in a sharp breath. Of course. In my shock of learning I had a brother and that my father had started a new family and then left Bo as well, I'd completely missed the fact that Bo's connection to Mia was a game changer. If Mia was anywhere in the southeastern part of Louisiana, we'd find her using a couple of drops of Bo's blood.

"It's that easy?" he asked, suspicion in his tone as he stuffed his hands in his pockets.

"Not easy exactly, but if all goes well, it could lead us to her." Jade tightened her grip on his hands and gazed up at him. "I, too, know what it's like to be abandoned. It's not something you ever get over; at least I haven't despite having found answers and peace in my life. But you can't let it define you. This moment, right now. It's one of those times that matter. Make sure you make it count." She pulled him in closer and gently placed a kiss on his cheek before she quietly retreated from the room.

Bo glanced over at me. "You trust her?"

"With my life," I said.

"Then let's do this."

# Chapter 23

THE COOL SPRING air sent a chill over my skin, but I barely noticed. We were once again back outside near the cypress tree, Jade at the northern point of the circle, me at the southern, with Bo and Miss Kitty at east and west.

"I really wish I had my camera set up for this," Miss Kitty said as Jade's magic flared to life. "My fans would die to see this."

"Miss Kitty, you know you can't talk about this on social media, right?" I said, reiterating Jade's stipulation for the woman to participate in the finding spell.

She waved a hand. "I already said I wouldn't, didn't I?"

"You did," I agreed. "Just making sure."

"It would mean big things for your café if I did though. Can you imagine the publicity? I heard that Mayhem Gator Tours is booked up for two months due to my Ida May video."

"That's true," Bo confirmed. "Reservations has been swamped for the past two days."

"The café is fine as it is," I said, but I couldn't help wondering if she was right. There was no doubt that people were highly fascinated with all things paranormal. If I branded the café the home of Ida May, it could help bring in more tourists.

"Can we focus, please?" Jade asked.

"Sorry." Miss Kitty snapped to attention as if she were a recruit in the military.

"What do you want me to do again?" Bo asked.

"When I finish the incantation, you'll need to make a small cut on your palm and let a couple of drops of blood spill into the earth."

He grimaced but nodded. "Okay. I'm ready."

"All right then. Let's find Mia." Static electricity filled the air as Jade unleashed her considerable power into the circle. My body started to hum with it, igniting that spark deep inside me. Once again I was alive, powerful, and reenergized after the long, emotional day. All the fatigue vanished, leaving me ready for anything.

Jade repeated the incantation she'd used earlier, only this time when she did, an invisible force overtook me, pulling my magic from me to combine with hers before slamming into Bo.

"Now!" she called, her arms wide and her head tilted to the darkened sky.

Bo, holding a small pocket knife, let out a hiss as he sliced open his palm. The light breeze vanished, and everything went eerily silent. Bo held his hand out, palm facing me, over our makeshift circle. I watched, transfixed, as a droplet of blood ran down his hand, pooled, and then finally fell in slow motion to the ground.

The second the blood hit the turf, Jade raised her hands and cried, "Mia! Hear my call. From water to stone and blood to bone, show us how to bring you home."

Nothing happened for a few beats, but then I felt it. The

ground rolled beneath my feet, followed by a low-pitched, inhuman moan, the kind I'd expect to hear in the engine room of a sinking ship.

"What's happening?" Bo asked in a panic.

Jade didn't answer. Her arms were out to the side, her head tilted back, power flowing from her like a broken water main.

"It's just… the… spell," I forced out, panting from the effort to stay upright. The magic being forced from me felt like a hundred-pound weight on my shoulders.

"This is amazing!" Miss Kitty called, mirroring Jade's stance, her purple-and-silver-streaked hair billowing out behind her.

"This is crazy!" Bo shouted just as the circle exploded with a giant pool of light, nearly blinding me.

I blinked, trying to focus, and squinted. It was nearly impossible to make out the dark shape darting around the circle. "What is that?"

"It's Mia," Jade said, her voice steady and clear.

I studied the shape but couldn't see anything other than a formless shadow. "How do you know?"

"I can feel her frustration. She wants to talk to us but can't."

"It's Emerson. He's spelled her. I know it!" Bo shouted. "Mia! It's me, Bo. Can you hear me?"

The blob shifted, growing larger, then smaller, then folding in on itself before it finally materialized into something sort of resembling the shape of a human. A young woman's face emerged from the shadows, her eyes wild. Her shapeless body spun from person to person until her gaze landed on Bo.

Then she started to scream.

"Mia!" Bo shouted again and fell to his knees, helpless and broken.

Mia's screams faded away along with her shadowed body, and all that was left was darkness.

Jade's connection to my magic severed instantly and the force of it pulled me forward, causing me to land face-first in the grass. I let out a grunt and rolled over, staring up into the dark sky.

"Bo?" I heard Jade ask tentatively.

"She's alive," he said, his voice shaky.

"Yes. She is. Now we need to make a plan."

"What plan?" He scoffed. "The spell didn't tell us anything."

"It told us plenty," Jade said. "We now know she's alive, has likely been cursed, and she's within a day's drive."

I pushed myself up, my head spinning.

"Need a hand?" Miss Kitty asked, kneeling beside me.

"I'm okay. I just need a second," I said, concentrating on my breathing. Was this how Jade felt after all her magical encounters? If so, that sucked donkey balls. Because dang. Talk about draining.

"Pyper?" Jade called.

I glanced up to find her motioning toward Bo. He was sitting in the middle of the circle where Mia had been, tears staining his cheeks as he held his head with both hands.

That ache in my chest came roaring back, making it nearly impossible to breathe. The pain that kid had suffered was unbearable. I crawled over to him and, without a word, wrapped my arms around him.

A small sob escaped his lips.

"It's going to be all right, Bo. I promise. We'll find her. We won't stop until we do."

He turned, buried his face in my shoulder, and cried softly.

✧  ✧  ✧

I LAY IN the bed I'd shared with Julius the past few days, with only Stella to snuggle me. Petting the little dog, I stared at the ceiling. It was just before dawn, and even though I'd gotten only a few hours of sleep, I was wide awake. I hadn't heard from Julius since he and Kane had taken Emerson to the council. But I had sent him a text letting him know we'd found Bo. Jade hadn't heard from Kane either. It was hard not to worry even though we both knew they could handle themselves.

Then there was Bo. After his breakdown in the magic circle, he'd disappeared into one of the other bedrooms. When I'd knocked to see if he was okay, he'd asked to be left alone. It had taken all my willpower to honor his wishes. I barely knew the kid, but my protective instincts had taken over while he'd cried in my arms. And I knew right then and there I'd do whatever it took to ensure he felt loved and safe for the rest of his life.

Stella wiggled out from under my hand and then moved to lie on my chest, her little head snuggled up on my neck. The weight of her body was comforting after such a trying day. "Hopefully we'll be going home soon, little one."

She let out a soft whine and gently pawed my cheek. Smiling down at her, I felt my eyes grow heavy. A moment later, I fell back into a fitful sleep.

✧  ✧  ✧

THE POUNDING ENTERED my consciousness just before I heard Julius's voice call, "Pyper, wake up!"

I bolted upright, blinking the sleep out of my eyes. "What it is?"

"It's Bo. He's gone." Julius threw a pair of black jeans at me. "Get dressed. We've got to go after him."

My heart leaped into my throat. What was he doing? Did he go to find Mia without us? Thirty seconds later, I was in my jeans, a light blue T-shirt, and my running shoes. "Any idea on where he went?"

"Miss Kitty thinks he went for coffee." Julius's bloodshot eyes darted around the room and finally landed on my dagger sitting on the nightstand. "Bring that."

"To do what? Stab the barista?" I joked. Even though I wasn't happy Bo had left the inn on his own, it was unlikely any of the bikers were up this early, waiting for him at the local café.

"You don't understand. Emerson escaped last night."

"What!" I grabbed the dagger and sheathed it against my hip. "Why didn't you tell me?"

"I called, but you didn't answer." He held the door open for me. "Kane is with Jade now, and Miss Kitty is downstairs talking to Ida May."

"Ida May? Is she in ghost or human form?" Not that it mattered either way. But I'd assumed that after she dissipated into dust the night before that she was back to her ghostly ways.

"Human. How did that happen?"

I scooped up Stella and headed out into the hallway. "Yesterday we did a finding spell for Bo and somehow she managed to feed off my magic and turn into her human form. But it wore off later in the evening. I'm not sure why she's back now."

I glanced back at him. "Did anyone fill you in on everything you missed?"

"No. Kane and I just got back about ten minutes ago. We sat down to have breakfast and before I took the first bite of my coffee cake, Miss Kitty came running in, arms waving about Bo being gone. Apparently she saw him leaving his bedroom, mumbling about coffee, but when she went to bring him a cup, he was nowhere to be found."

"Dammit! Well, there's only one way to find out." We stopped in the kitchen where I deposited Stella on Ida May's lap.

She grinned up at me. "Don't I look pretty this morning?"

I eyed the black leather corset, lace skirt, and knee-high boots. "Where did you get those?"

"In Moxie's closet. When I woke up like this"—she waved a hand down her body—"I figured it wouldn't hurt to borrow them since she left town. You don't think she'd mind do you?"

"You just woke up in human form?" I asked, skeptical.

"Yep. Isn't it great? Now I can do that interview with Miss Kitty. I'm going to be an Internet star!"

"Great. Just make sure you feed Stella and take her on a walk." I didn't wait for her to answer before I turned to Kane and Jade. "We're going to go look for Bo at the café. Text us if he shows up."

"You got it," Jade said.

Kane stood and walked us to the back door. "Be careful, okay?"

"We will," I said, patting my dagger. "I'm armed and dangerous now."

My best friend's eyes flashed with pride. "That's my girl."

# Chapter 24

I QUICKLY FILLED Julius in on the revelation that Bo and Mia were siblings and that Bo was my brother.

"Wow. That's remarkable," he said, tightening his grip on my hand.

"Yeah. It's a little overwhelming."

He glanced down at me as we crossed the street, heading toward Bettie's Beignets. "It also explains why that finding spell I used right after he was abducted attached itself to you when it lost his trail."

Holy hell, I'd forgotten all about that. He was right. I was about to say something about it when my phone dinged with a text. It was from Bo.

*I know where Mia is. Meet me at Otis's camp ASAP. Miss Kitty knows where it is.*

"Ohmigod! How is he getting there? Dammit." I showed the text to Julius and then typed one of my own. *Where are you? Meet us back at the house. We'll go together. Emerson escaped.*

I bit down on my bottom lip as Julius and I hurried back to the inn. "Why isn't he texting me back?"

Julius frowned. "He's probably too wound up to think clearly. He just found out Mia's alive after she's been missing for five years. Can you blame him?"

"No. But that doesn't mean he should go off by himself when we're here to help. And what about Otis? Does Bo really think that sweet old man is holding her captive?"

Julius gave me a hardened look. "You never know who people are until they reveal themselves."

I stared up at him, wanting to push back, to yell, to tell him he was wrong. But I couldn't. Because time and time again, people I'd thought could be trusted turned out to be psychopaths. Finally I shook my head in exasperation and then stormed into the inn, more worried than upset.

"Miss Kitty!" I called.

"Yes, dear?" The older woman poked her head out of the pantry.

"We need to get to Otis's camp. Can you give me directions?"

She stepped out of the walk-in closet, her hands full of plastic Ziploc bags. "I'm sorry. No. You'd never find it. I'll just have to show you."

"I don't think—What are you holding?" The bags in her hands had one item each and they looked like... voodoo dolls?

"The cat was playing with them. I found two in the pantry, one in the upstairs bathroom, and another in the living room. I didn't want anyone to accidently touch them. These things are dangerous. I mean, this one here? It's Bubble, Bubble, Crotch Rot, and Trouble. I don't know what Moxie was doing with these, but this right here? It takes the saying 'digging for gold' to a whole new level."

"Oh for the love of...," Julius said.

I clasped my hand over my mouth to muffle the laugh and

sputtered, "That's not funny."

"Yes it is, or you wouldn't be laughing." She placed the plastic bags on the counter. "Now, what's this about getting to Otis's camp?"

"Right. Bo is there. He thinks that's where he's going to find Mia."

"I'll grab my keys." She spun, ready to run upstairs.

"Wait," Julius called.

She paused and turned back.

"No need to drive. We'll take Kane's SUV. Besides, it's probably not a good idea to drive yours around right now."

"Right." She calmly walked back over to the counter and picked up the plastic bags.

"What are you doing with those?" I asked.

"Just in case one of those bikers tries to get handsy like they did last night. Cursing them with crotch rot would be poetic justice."

"Okay then." I turned to Julius. "Tell Jade and Kane we're ready."

✧   ✧   ✧

KANE TURNED THE Lexus SUV down a narrow dirt road and cringed when the overgrown vegetation scraped against the paint.

"That's what insurance is for, honey," Jade said, patting his knee.

He let out a long sigh. "We just got it back from the body shop from the last situation."

Being a demon hunter meant Kane usually couldn't go a day without getting into some sort of altercation. It was to be expected. "I told you to buy the used Jeep," I said, still wondering why he'd dropped so much money on a car he knew would get trashed.

"This one has better handling." Kane tightened his hands around the wheel and swerved to the right to miss a giant pothole full of water and managed to end up with a grill full of wisteria.

"Good one, Mario Andretti," I said.

Jade, who was riding in the front passenger seat, snickered, but when Kane gave her an irritated look, she quieted down. Still, she glanced over her shoulder and sent me an amused smile.

"The camp is down the road to the left," Miss Kitty said. She sat to my right, her face plastered to the window. Julius was on my left, leaving me to ride in the middle.

Everyone went silent as we waited for the camp to come into view. Bo still hadn't texted me back, and my gut was starting to churn. I'd somehow managed to ward off the anxiety long enough to get through the car ride, but now that we were almost there...

"Stop the car," Jade said. "See ahead? Looks like we have company."

"Crap," I muttered, eyeing the half dozen motorcycles and familiar black SUV.

"We've got this," Jade said, all business now. "Three witches, a demon hunter, and Miss Kitty. No one is taking us down." She opened her door and hopped out, already making her way toward the camp. Kane quickly followed.

"You should stay here," I told Miss Kitty.

"No way!" She jerked her door open, clutched her large

shoulder bag, and before I managed to slide out, she was already running after Jade.

"Great." I made my way around to where Julius was waiting for me. "Someone has to keep an eye on her."

"Well will, but I have a feeling she knows how to take care of herself."

"Probably, but if we end up in a magical battle…" I couldn't even finish the thought. "Why didn't we think to bring Ida May?"

"I'm right here," she said from behind me.

I spun around and my jaw dropped when I spotted her in her Victoria vixen outfit. "How did you get here?"

"Ghost, remember?" She winked and jerked her head toward the camp. "I'll make sure the kitten doesn't get into too much trouble."

Julius and I followed as she ran to catch up to Miss Kitty. There was no point in trying to be stealthy. There was only one way into the camp. Quietly sneaking up on them was out of the question. Going in guns blazing was pretty much our only choice. Not that I minded. If Emerson Charles was here, I was more than ready to bring him down.

We heard the first sounds of battle before we saw it. Jade yelled out a warning, and a loud crackle of magic followed. Grunts and shouts rang through the bayou. When we cut through a line of trees, we spotted Jade and Kane fighting off what appeared to be an army of bikers. But neither Bo nor Emerson was among them. And there was no woman in sight.

"This way." I tugged on Julius's arm and took off for the stairs leading to the raised cabin. I was halfway up before I realized Julius wasn't with me. He'd gotten caught in the magical battle below, helping Jade fight off a tag team of bikers who were lobbing green ooze in their direction. One blob hit the dirt near Julius's feet and burned a hole in the earth instantly.

"Go!" Julius called. "We've got this."

I didn't hesitate. If Bo was in there, I had to get him out. I burst through the door and came to an abrupt stop. Emerson Charles stood right in the middle of the room. Bo was pressed up against the wall, watching his every movement.

But a woman who looked to be close to my own age, stood between them, her hands spread wide. She had thick, wavy, black hair that nearly reached her butt; big, round, ice-blue eyes; and was dressed in jeans, an off-the-shoulder red blouse, and silver high heels. Silver bangles climbed one arm, and big silver hoops were in her ears. All she needed was the designer bag and she'd have been ready for her cover on a fashion magazine.

"Stay away from my brother, Emerson," the woman who had to be Mia said. "You already have half the county as your minions. You don't need him too."

"Clearly I do if I'm to keep you in line," he shot back, stalking toward her.

Neither had so much as glanced in my direction. I couldn't tell if they knew I was there or not.

Emerson reached out and grabbed her by the neck, lifting her a couple of inches off the floor. Bo rushed forward as I reached for my dagger. Adrenaline rushed through me, igniting the growingly familiar magic inside me.

"Put me down, Emerson," Mia ordered.

Her words made me pause. Someone who was being choked shouldn't have been able to speak so clearly. I studied her.

Emerson's hand was indeed wrapped around her neck. His knuckles were going white with the force of his grip. But she appeared unaffected, as if he wasn't even there at all.

"You son of a bitch!" Bo cried and tackled Emerson.

"Bo! No!" Mia landed easily on her feet, but Emerson and Bo crashed to the floor. Bo landed a punch to Emerson's temple that had the biker rolling and scrambling to get away from him.

I moved in, blue magic racing up and down my dagger.

But Emerson, who never even looked back at me, shot a bolt of magic right at my chest. On reflex, I brought the knife up, barely managing to block the spell before it blasted me across the room. The electric power crashed into the wall, sending splinters of rough wood across the room.

"You ungrateful little bastard," Emerson snarled at Bo. "This is what I get for taking you in after your father abandoned you?"

"You think you get credit for giving me a cot and letting me make you your meals? Or for running tourists around the bayou when all you ever paid me was gas money? And the whole time you've had my sister locked away in this camp, cultivating your special pot plants and mixing hallucinogens? You're sick."

Pot? Hallucinogens? Emerson wasn't just running a chop shop but manufacturing drugs too? I glanced through the open door of the kitchen and spotted a long table full of herbs, mason jars, plastic bags, and scales. I'd been so focused on Mia and Bo when I'd come in, I hadn't even noticed. Jeez. What had we stumbled into?

"You need to shut your mouth, boy."

Bo's face turned a dark shade of maroon, and he once again lunged for Emerson. But the biker was too fast. His hands came up and he shot raw power at Bo.

"No!" Ida May materialized out of nowhere, solid and once again in human form, and took the electric magic right in the chest. She froze, her eyes wide and her mouth open in an *O* shape. Everyone stilled as we watched her body turn to ash, then vanish into thin air.

Even though I knew she was a ghost, it was still jarring to see her erased so completely. My ire rose to unbearable levels, and I clutched my knife harder.

"You destroyed her!" Bo raged and swung, bashing the big biker in the side of the head.

Emerson stumbled sideways, grabbed a nearby wood chair, and hurled it at Bo. The teenager was too agile though and leaped over it right onto Emerson.

Mia and I both ran to help Bo, but Emerson let out a roar and threw Bo into the wall. His head hit the wood siding with a sick thunk, and he slid down the wall in slow motion, crumpling when he hit the floor.

Holy hell. If we didn't stop Emerson, he was going to kill Bo. I was certain of it. Mia skidded to a stop and retreated back to Bo. But I didn't. With each thunderous beat of my heart, my magic built. It coursed under my skin, itching to be used.

Running forward, I raised the knife, determined to stop him one way or another, but when I was two steps away, Emerson flung his hand out toward me. An invisible force field appeared, keeping me trapped and helpless on the other side.

"Mia!" I cried, getting her attention.

She glanced up from her position where she was crouched beside Bo, holding his head as she whispered to him.

"Get him out of here," I yelled.

SPIRITS, BEIGNETS, AND A BAYOU BIKER GANG

Too late. Emerson grabbed her by the ankle, spun her around, and sent her flying into the nearest wall. She hit and bounced right back on her feet, already moving toward him.

*"Consto!"* he shouted, pointing at her.

She froze midstep, her eyes narrowed and fists clenched.

"Damn you, Emerson!"

He ignored me and stalked over to Bo.

I banged on the solid force field, and when all I did was bounce off, I clutched my knife, took a few steps back, and then rushed the wall, dagger raised. The moment the tip pierced the invisible wall, fiery pain shot up my arm. I screamed, the agony nearly making me pass out.

"Pyper!" I heard Julius call from behind me, then felt a cooling sensation splash over me as if I'd been doused in cold water.

My dagger clattered to the floor, only mere inches from Emerson's reach.

"No," I breathed.

Julius's strong arms wrapped around my waist, steadying me. "I got you."

I glanced up into his green eyes and was almost knocked over with the concern shining back at me. "Thanks," I said, already spinning out of his embrace as I heard Emerson start a chant.

Mia was still frozen in place. Bo was propped up against the wall, trying and failing to get to his feet. He was hurt. A knee or ankle since he wasn't able to put any weight on his right leg.

Mist rose up around Emerson as he reached down and picked up *my* dagger. With pure evil shining back at me, he met my eyes and placed the dagger against his palm. Then he turned toward Bo and started the incantation. "Bound by blood, bound by bone, let my offering be the promise that you will never be alone."

"Binding spell," Julius gasped out and ran forward, his powerful magic lighting up his hands. Emerson saw him and once again sent the invisible force field up. Julius didn't let it stop him. His magic blew a hole in it with no trouble, sending a million tiny little cracks through it until it shattered. Live magic flew through the air, a good portion of it landing on Mia. The second the magic cloud hit her, she sucked in a gasp of air, her chest heaving.

"Whoa." That amount of magic should've been deadly. But she had survived it. How? And if she was that powerful, what had kept her here for so long? A binding spell, or fealty? She sure hadn't seemed like she was following orders.

"Blood and bone, blood and bone," Emerson chanted, magic radiating off him in waves. "From now until the end of days, your heart is as cold as stone." Black ropes of magic spewed from his fingertips, snaking their way toward Bo.

I sucked in a sharp gasp and turned to Julius. "We need Jade." She was the only one I knew who could fight black magic and win.

"Go!" Julius pointed toward the door as he moved to somehow help my brother. But before I got to the door, I heard Mia's high-pitched scream and turned around just in time to see her jump in front of the black ropes.

I clasped my hand over my mouth to keep from crying out and watched as the ropes slid easily into her, winding and twisting and invading every part of her until her eyes went pure black. Then she rose in the air, palms out, long hair flying behind her.

"You stupid—" Emerson was cut off by her scream.

Mia's mouth opened, and the black smoke vines came pouring out, wrapped around her body, and tightened. She went silent and hung there for a second, her big, round black eyes seeing nothing. Then her body turned to ash, just like Ida May's had. The particles floated down but vanished before they hit the floor.

Mia was gone. Just like Ida May. That could mean only one thing: Mia was a ghost.

# Chapter 25

"M IA!" BO CALLED from his spot against the wall. He forced himself to his feet, leaning heavily against the wall to save putting weight on his right leg. "You killed her!"

Emerson shrugged. "Five years ago, but she's bound to me, so she'll be back soon enough. And you'll be right here waiting for her."

Julius and I shared a glance. Black magic was nothing to be messing with. Finding Jade would be ideal, but the fact that she hadn't made it up to the camp meant she was still handling things below. I gestured to the door and mouthed her name, but Julius shook his head. Instead, he pulled out an item I'd forgotten about completely.

The jar of green slush he'd gotten from Avrilla that day at the Swamp Witch. Then he produced the gator claws and tossed them to me. I studied them, wondering what I was supposed to do with them, trying to recall what Avrilla had said. *For protection.*

Emerson held my knife up, pointing it toward Bo. "You're turning out to be more trouble than you're worth."

"So kill me too then," Bo shouted. "I don't have anybody anyway."

My heart seized, and suddenly it was hard to breathe. I'd just found him, and the fact that he was ready to surrender to his abuser was more than I could process. I ran forward and put myself between them. "You have me, Bo. Always. And I'm not letting anyone get in the way of my knowing my little brother."

"Brother?" Emerson scoffed. "You're related to that trash?"

"You're the only one here who's trash. Now back off before I stab you with that dagger." I nodded to the knife in his hand, forcing my bravado. How I was going to get it away from him, I had no idea, but I was tired of being afraid of the bully. I tightened my grip on the alligator claws and waited for his next move.

He raised the dagger, inspecting it, then held it out to me as if taunting me to come and get it. Before I could do anything, he flicked his fingers at me as if I were an annoying bug. But the force behind the magic that followed slammed into my gut, bounced off, and left me relatively unharmed, as if I were wearing a Kevlar vest designed specifically for magic.

"What did you do?" he roared, moving toward me.

"Nothing." But the gator claws in my hand had turned to dust, and I knew Avrilla's advice had saved my life. I narrowed my eyes and gazed over his shoulder at Julius. He had the jar open, and the green goo was oozing out in a noxious cloud. The stench made me gag, but more importantly, it distracted Emerson.

He glanced over his shoulder, and whatever he saw made him drop his guard just long enough for me to rush him. Calling on my self-defense training, I grabbed his wrist, twisted it behind his back, and pushed him forward so he was leaning down. Total rookie move, but he'd been unprepared and dropped the dagger at my feet.

"You bit—"

Without hesitation, I brought my elbow down on his neck with so much force we both went down. He thrashed while I rolled, reaching for the hilt of my dagger. The cool metal hit my palm, igniting my magic and sending me bouncing up on the balls of my feet. My heart thundered, and it took me a moment to process what I saw.

Emerson was still on the floor, but the green gas had cleared. I blinked, certain my eyes were playing tricks on me.

But no. They weren't.

Avrilla had emerged from the green gas and was now standing over Emerson, one spiked heel positioned against his neck. "It's time to say good-bye, Emerson," she said, her voice calm, almost soothing. "Your days of torturing my children are over."

"Mom?" Bo asked, his voice full of awe.

I glanced between the two, understanding and wonder sending chills up my spine. Avrilla was a ghost as well and had done everything in her power to help free her daughter and to save Bo from his inevitable fate.

"Hi, honey." She smiled at him, but when Emerson jerked, she pressed harder, her heel appearing dangerously close to his carotid artery.

"Go ahead, Avrilla. That might slow me down, but it won't kill me," he said with a growl.

"No, but this will." She pulled an identical dagger to mine out of her dress pocket, and in one swift movement she slammed it into his back. He lit up with blue light but didn't freeze as he had when I'd stabbed him. Instead, he rose up, and with rage in his dark eyes he took one look at her, then turned and unleashed a massive amount of power into Bo's chest.

My brother rose off the ground, suspended by the magic, his body convulsing as if he were being electrocuted. His eyes rolled into the back of his head and his skin turned gray.

"Bo!" Avrilla screamed and reached for him, but the moment Emerson's power touched her, she vanished.

Instinct took over, and although I sensed Julius calling on an incredible force of power, I was already moving. Magic so powerful, so incredibly intense, vibrated through me, and when I leaped, I literally flew across the room and buried the knife in Emerson's heart.

The biker went completely still, then fell with a loud crash.

I landed gracefully on my feet, dagger still in hand. It was then I realized I'd never let go. I stared down at the man who suddenly looked ashen. His eyes were sunken and his hair had turned gray. There was no blue magic keeping him in limbo. No dagger still in his chest. Nothing.

I'd killed him.

My dagger fell to the floor as I started to tremble. My knees gave out, and I would have crumpled to the floor if Julius hadn't caught me.

"Hey," he said softly. "You're okay. Everything is okay."

I leaned into his chest but then jerked back. "Bo!"

"He's going to be fine too." Julius turned us both so I could see Bo sitting up with Avrilla beside him. She had her arms around him and was holding him in much the same way Julius was holding me.

"Thank the goddess," I breathed.

"You were amazing," Julius said softly. "Incredible."

I shook my head, tears stinging my eyes. I'd done something no person should ever have to do.

"You did it. Oh my god, I'm free!" A woman's voice pulled me out of my pit of despair, and I looked up to find Mia floating in the middle of the room, Ida May next to her, beaming at me.

"Way to go, Pyper," Ida May said. "I really wanted to be the one to ice that a-hole, but if it wasn't me, I'm happy it was you. Us NOLA girls really know how to get the job done."

I refrained from rolling my eyes. It wasn't like I hadn't had a metric crap ton of help. If Avrilla hadn't given me the dagger, instead of being an asset I'd have been a casualty. "So do the bayou girls," I said, giving Mia a bittersweet smile. "I'm sorry we weren't able to find you sooner."

She gave me an odd look. "How long have you been looking?"

"Two, three days?" I couldn't even remember how much time had passed since I'd first talked to Sterling. "We should've gotten here sooner."

"Why?" She glanced at Avrilla and Bo. Avrilla was staring off in another direction while Bo rested his head against her shoulder. Then she turned her attention back to me. "What would you have changed?"

I waved a hand at her. "Look at you. If we'd found you earlier, you wouldn't be a ghost right now."

Her brow furrowed. "Pyper, I've been a ghost for five years."

"But I thought..." I glanced at Avrilla. "Sterling said she was still alive." It dawned on me Emerson had said he'd killed Mia, but for some reason my brain hadn't registered that piece of information as truth. Why would it? Sterling had told me she was alive.

Avrilla shook her head slowly. "I'm sorry. We didn't think you'd work as hard to save her if you knew she was dead."

I stood up, and Julius mirrored my movement. "You can't be serious. You put us through all this when there was no hope of saving her? We put our lives on the line for lies!"

The swamp witch got to her feet, and with no apology reflected in either her stature or her tone, she said, "Mia was a prisoner here. Emerson Charles put a binding spell on her before she died. Before *he* killed her. And it stuck with her in death. Because of her witch bloodline, she has the ability to appear human quite a bit of the time—just like I do—and because of that, he forced her to run his drug trade. I couldn't stand the thought of letting her exist in such a state for however long Emerson Charles managed to live. I've been searching for the right person to help her for almost five years."

"And I was it?" I asked, incredulous.

She nodded. "You had… something. It was a feeling I couldn't describe. But deep in my gut, I knew you'd save my daughter. Now I know why." She glanced back at Bo, who was staring at all of us with fascination. "It's your connection to Bo."

I blew out a breath. Her explanation made perfect sense. And had I been in her shoes, I'd have done what I had to as well. But the thing is, I'd have tried to help her knowing she was a ghost. It was what I did.

"Not to mention, that dagger chose you," she added.

"What do you mean?" I tilted my head.

"I had two. My grandmother gave them both to me. She was a powerful swamp witch, one of the most powerful around, and she spelled them. She said they help unlock one's true potential. Mine used to be as powerful as yours… until they day I died. Then when you walked into my shop, the second one spoke to me. It chose you. It's why you were able to end Emerson and I wasn't."

"But I stabbed him before and that didn't happen then," I said, confused.

"Apart, the daggers are powerful. Together they are deadly." She picked up the mahogany-handled dagger—hers—and handed it to Bo. "This is yours now. Use it wisely."

He ran his gaze over it, not saying a word, then nodded and took the knife in hand. A faint trace of blue magic skittered over the blade.

Avrilla smiled. "When the time is right, the dagger will be there for you."

Bo cast his gaze at Emerson, still lying ashen and unmoving on the floor. "Did he kill you?"

Avrilla nodded. "Poisoned me in my shop. It's where I've been ever since."

My hatred for the man rose up again. Pure evil.

"He always wanted to possess me, to force me to work for him," she continued, suddenly desperate to explain everything to her son. "When I refused, he finally got his revenge. But it didn't stop there. He went after Mia, knowing she had my skills. I imagine that's why he went after you too. Only it didn't occur to me he would if he had Mia."

"But I don't have magic," Bo said, fingering the dagger.

"Not yet. I imagine he was betting on you growing into your skills."

Bo nodded. "Probably."

And even if Bo never was able to use magic, that likely wouldn't have mattered much to Emerson. He'd already been grooming the kid to be an indentured servant. Either way, he couldn't lose. Until Avrilla and Sterling sent me to help. A small amount of pride welled in my chest at the thought I was the reason Bo was finally safe.

Bo turned to meet his mother's bittersweet gaze. "Mom?"

"Yes?" She ran her hand over his head the way only mothers could.

"Why have you not visited me? I know Mia was trapped here. But couldn't you have warned me or something? I mean, I know you're, uh… dead, but if you're here now…"

Her smile turned sad. "I was trapped in my shop. A controlling spell by Emerson, the same one that forced Mia to stay here. But then today, when Julius used the spell I gave him for protection, it brought me here… to you."

My heart was going to crack in two. Her love was so fierce, so unending. She'd have done anything for her children and had. I held my hand out to Julius. He stepped up and slipped his fingers over mine, squeezing gently.

"Pyper?" Mia said.

I turned to give her my attention. She was still floating, almost completely transparent, and about to fade out for however long it took her to recharge. "Yes?"

"Will you give Bo a message for me?"

I started to nod, then stopped and waved toward him. "He's right there."

"I know. But he can't hear me. My energy is too depleted."

I studied everyone's confused expressions and realized it was only me who could hear her. "I see. In that case, I can do one better than that. But there are ground rules."

"For a message?" she asked.

"No. For how you're going to deliver it." I winked at Julius as he stifled a sigh. I knew what he was going to say: that just because I could do something didn't mean I had to. But in this case, I did. Bo was my brother, and if I could give him this gift, the risks were worth it. "Okay, here's the thing. I've recently learned that I can 'host' spirits in my body for short periods of time if I invite them."

"What does that mean?" she asked.

"Exactly what it sounds like. I'm offering my body as a vessel for you to speak directly to Bo. If you want."

Her eyes lit up, and she bobbed up and down as if she were jumping with excitement.

I grinned. "The rules are you can't take up residence in my body. And when and if I ask you to leave, you leave. Got it?"

"Yes. Absolutely."

"Good. Ready?"

"What do I need to do?" she asked.

"Not much. Just think about how much you want to talk to Bo. And when I say now, walk straight into my body."

I turned to face my brother.

His eyes were huge. "You're talking to her right now?"

"Yes. And in a second, you will be too."

Avrilla tightened her hold on him, clutching almost desperately. I knew that that her time with us was limited too. At least the three of them would have this moment.

I took a deep, cleansing breath and closed my eyes. When I opened them, I said, "Now, Mia."

She floated toward me, barely a whisper of an image. A

stinging chill ran up my spine when we joined but was quickly replaced by a warmth I recognized as joy.

"Mom? Bo?" she said softly and moved toward them.

I retreated to that place in my mind where I sat on my metaphorical couch, looking down on them as they hugged and cried and held on to each other. Promises were made to visit Bo and to keep an eye out for him. And they all laughed when he stared at them in horror and asked, "You aren't going to be watching *all* the time are you?"

Avrilla nodded and laughed. "*All* the time. Remember that and behave accordingly."

"Gross, Mother," Mia added and turned to Bo. "Don't worry. I'll make sure she gives you your privacy. Just as long as you aren't a douche."

Shortly after, they all fell silent. Then Bo asked, "What am I going to do now?"

"Pyper will watch over you," Avrilla said. "Listen to her. She has a good heart."

At the mention of my name, that warmth spread over me again. Mia's voice sounded in my head, *On the first day of the season, Bo will find his strength, his courage, and his inner light. Be there to guide him.*

"Wha...?" I started to ask, but stopped when I realized Mia had vanished right after she'd shared her vision with me. She'd seen Bo come into his own, and she'd asked that I help him.

Which meant Bo had magic. I wanted to share his sister's words with him, but his pained expression stopped me. He wasn't ready. Not now, and maybe not even until his powers manifested.

In the next minute I was sitting on the floor next to Bo, his mother and sister gone. "They'll be back," I said.

"You think so?" His voice cracked and his shoulders hunched as he stared at the floor.

"I know so."

# Chapter 26

"HOW DID YOU know Mia was here?" I asked Bo as we descended the steps to where Jade and Miss Kitty were waiting for us.

He stuffed his hands in his pockets. "Emerson has been renting this place from Otis for as long as I can remember. Twice a week for the past two years, part of my job was to make deliveries. Emerson told me they were fishing & hunting supplies for the club members, but I knew better. No one goes through that much ammo and bait. It had to be supplies for Mia to manufacture his drugs."

Of course Emerson would put someone on the task who was an insider. And who better than a kid who ran gator tours? "Kind of risky since Mia was here."

"I suppose he figured it didn't matter if I did find out. But as it was, I only saw her twice, both times brief, and she disappeared right after. I chalked it up to hallucinating. But when you said she was alive…" He swallowed. "The memories came back to me while I was trying to get to sleep, and I just couldn't wait. I'm sorry I caused so much trouble."

I wrapped my arm around his shoulders and pulled him in. "You didn't. There was going to be trouble no matter what went down."

He nodded and fell silent as we reached Miss Kitty and Jade. They were both a little worse for the wear. Miss Kitty's gold boots were caked with mud, and her gold belt was missing completely. Jade's hair resembled a bird's nest, sticking out in all directions. She had soot clinging to her skin, and her jeans had burn holes.

"I'd hate to see what the other guys look like," I said, eyeing them.

Miss Kitty started laughing. "You'd enjoy the one walking like a duck. That chafing voodoo doll really did a number on him. I'd say it's going to be a while before he can squeeze back into his leather riding pants."

My eyebrows shot up. "You used the voodoo dolls on them?"

"Absolutely. A girl has to use the tools allotted to her. That vile one who shoved me in the mud and ruined my boots? Not even a doctor is going to be able to help him with his bacne."

Jade nodded. "It was something out of a horror movie. I think I'd rather have been cursed with the crotch rot one."

Miss Kitty snorted. "Oh no, dear. The jackhole who was blessed with that one actually threw himself in the bayou. Last I saw him he was trying to outswim a water moccasin."

I shuddered.

She shrugged. "Life is hard in the bayou. Harder when you cross Miss Kitty."

Jade laughed and I giggled.

She beamed at us, obviously pleased with herself.

"Where's Kane?" I asked her.

"Making sure the rest of the hikers are detained. Julius?"

"Talking to the council. They're sending a squad before local authorities get involved. It's a pretty big embarrassment for them, letting such a huge operation go undetected for so long."

Jade's lips thinned into a flat line. "They should be embarrassed. Let's just hope they listen to Julius the next time he warns them of a problem."

"And that they fix their security issues." There was no excuse for Emerson's escape. The council's supernatural holding cells were supposed to be the equivalent of the highest-level maximum-security prisons.

She glanced at me, suspicion in her expression. "I hate to say it, but it sounds like an inside job."

"Oh jeez. Don't say that. All I want to do is go home and enjoy the Quarter for a while."

She smiled. "And help your *brother* decorate his new room."

"Decorate?" Bo grimaced. "Just a mattress is fine."

I shook my head. "I think we can do better than that. You'll need a new rug, curtains, a comforter, and a desk to start."

He groaned. "It's been less than twenty-four hours since she found out we're siblings, and she's already telling me what to do."

I smiled up at him, my brilliant blue eyes mirrored in his. "I have some catching up to do."

✧   ✧   ✧

"I DON'T NEED any more crap for the bed," Bo complained from where he sat at his desk in what used to be my spare bedroom.

I shoved a pillow into the sham and tossed it against the headboard. "Of course you do. What if you're sitting on the bed doing your homework? You're going to want something to lean on."

"I'll sit here at the desk," he muttered and went back to typing on his computer.

"Right." I rolled my eyes and went to work on the second sham. "How's school?"

"Fine."

"And Madison?"

He spun around in the chair and narrowed his eyes at me. "How did you know about her?"

I gave him a sly smile. "I'm your sister. I know everything."

"You *think* you do anyway."

"You'll see." I smoothed the navy-and-brown comforter and was just about to fluff the throw pillows when a buzzer went off, indicating we had a visitor. Stella instantly went into attack mode, barking her head off in the other room.

"Saved, finally." Bo moaned, but the smile tugging at his lips gave him away.

"You love me," I said and strode out.

"Hale and Moxie are here," Julius said, still standing near the intercom. "They're on the way up."

"Really? I thought they weren't coming into town until the weekend." I glanced around at my living room. The mocha couches looked nice, but Julius and Bo had left their breakfast plates, two glasses, and a mug on the coffee table along with a stack of comic books. And Bo's grungy tennis shoes and smelly socks were strewn on the floor. I groaned. "My place used to be so tidy before I let you boys move in."

"But you also had a leaky faucet, a squeaky bathroom door, and two windows that wouldn't open. All fixed thanks to yours truly," he said, his chest puffed up in male pride.

"All things I could've either had Kane fix or hired a handyman for half a day's wages."

"True, but then you wouldn't have anyone to share your obsession with *American Horror Story*, give you shoulder rubs, or cook you dinner," he added.

All things neither Kane or Jade were interested in doing. He had a point. It turned out Bo and I had the same taste in television shows. We'd already binge-watched the first two seasons of *American Horror Story* and had a date to start the next one this upcoming weekend. And Julius, goddess love him, he'd decided to take cooking lessons and had been delighting us both with fancy dinners ranging from duck tacos to crawfish potpies. And the shoulder rubs, well, that usually started behind closed doors after Bo had shut himself in his bedroom for the night.

"Okay, you might have a point."

I quickly gathered up the dirty dishes while Julius tossed Bo's shoes and socks in his room. And by the time we both made it back into the living room, Moxie and Hale were already knocking on the door.

I pulled the door open and smiled at the pair we hadn't seen since they'd driven off for parts unknown. They were both relaxed and smiling, Moxie in a sundress and Hale in jeans and a T-shirt.

Holding the door open, I waved them in. "Hey! This is a surprise."

"Sorry to drop in on you like this, but it's sort of urgent," Moxie said, leaning in to give me a hug.

Foreboding settled over me. "What happened?"

"Oh!" Moxie shook her head and waved her arms. "Nothing

life and death. Nobody's been kidnapped or anything."

"That's good," Bo said, leaning in the doorway of his bedroom.

"Bo!" Moxie crossed the room, her arms out. "I'm so glad to see you. Is Pyper taking good care of you? How's school? Any girlfriends yet?"

"Moxie," Hale said. "Leave the kid alone. He's fine." Hale offered me his hand, and when I took it, he added, "It's nice to see you again, Pyper." He glanced over my shoulder at Julius. "You too, man."

Julius waved and uttered a greeting.

Bo shook his head in exasperation at Moxie, then hugged her. "I'm fine. Pyper's a pain in the butt though. Julius does his best to keep her in line, but even he can't stop her when she gets a bug up her—"

I cleared my throat. "I didn't see you complaining when I managed to get your schedule changed so that you could take that music class you wanted."

He clamped his mouth shut but couldn't stop his amused smiled. "True. Sometimes you're useful."

"Gee, thanks." I cast him an annoyed look, but when I turned back to Moxie, I was grinning. Sparring with my brother had turned into one of my favorite pastimes.

"Looks like y'all are settling in," she said on a laugh as she bent to scoop Stella up. The shih tzu wagged her tail and went on an excessive licking spree, covering Moxie's face in kisses.

"We're doing okay," I said. "Now, what can we help you with?"

"Right." Moxie put Stella down on the floor.

The little dog immediately made a beeline for Bo. While she

had an affinity for both me and Ida May—Stella loved playing with the ghost when she made surprise appearances—apparently the dog had decided Bo was her person. And as far as I was concerned, that was perfect. Both of them needed a lot of love and healing.

"Hale?" Moxie held her hand out.

The tall man rummaged around in a paper bag he was carrying and produced a plastic bag with a familiar-looking doll in it. He handed it to me and said, "I've been told you might know how to deactivate these."

I grabbed the bag, inspected it, and let out a gasp of surprise. The tag read: *Impotent Gentleman of Verona*. "Where did you find this?"

"Buried between the sheets in our bed. At first we thought someone cursed us intentionally, but then we found the cat playing with two more. He was in the process of ripping the packaging open on one that causes premature hair loss." She patted her hair and shuddered at the thought. "We were able to dispose of it before anyone was cursed. But this one… Ah, we're pretty sure it's why Hale can't—"

"Oh man. This is not what I need to hear." Bo disappeared back into his bedroom and slammed the door.

I stifled a laugh and tried to keep a straight face as I asked, "You think you've been hit with an ED curse?"

"Yes," Moxie said, letting out an exaggerated sigh. "When Miss Kitty explained everything that went down with Emerson, she mentioned the voodoo dolls and her role in helping take down the motorcycle gang. So I knew you'd picked some up at the Swamp Witch. I just had no idea we'd find one in our bed."

"Oh my," I said, covering my mouth in embarrassed horror.

"You don't think we had anything to do with cursing you, do you? We would never... I mean, those were a joke purchase for Jade."

"Gosh, no. Not at all. That cat of mine is mischievous to the core. If anyone is guilty, it's him. We just need to figure out how to lift the curse. I mean, it's been weeks now since, um... Well, let's just say we've been doing a lot of experimenting once I figured out Hale wasn't having an affair on me." She laughed uncomfortably but soldiered on. "That's why we'd been fighting you know. I mean, Hale is a machine. Never had any issue with his—"

"Moxie," Hale said, a slight edge in his tone. "Maybe they don't need *all* the details?"

"Right. Anyway. Can you help us?"

I couldn't stop myself. I chuckled. "Sure. I have just the thing. Follow me."

"Hale too?" she asked.

I shook my head. "No, all we need is the doll."

Moxie followed me into my bedroom where I retrieved my dagger and a shallow cardboard box I'd left in a pile from my recent online shopping spree. Her eyes went wide as I placed the doll, bag and all, inside the box and then pressed the tip of my dagger to the doll's would-be heart.

"Ready?" I asked.

"Is this going to hurt Hale?" she leaned in and whispered, "Or any of his parts? I could probably live without, well, you know, but—"

"He'll be fine. Better than fine. He won't feel a thing. Trust me."

She nodded but glanced over her shoulder toward the door.

"Here goes nothing," I said, and sliced the head off the voodoo doll. His actual head, not his other one.

Nothing seemed to happen at first, but then Hale called from the other room, "Moxie!"

"Oh my gosh. He's hurt." She hurried back into the living room, her movements jerky and slightly panicked. "Are you okay?" Before he managed to say anything, she placed her hand right on his crotch and said, "Did the spell—Oh!"

He grinned down at her. "We're back in business, baby."

She squealed while he grabbed her by the wrist and tugged her toward the door.

"Tell Bo we said good-bye," she said, waving as they disappeared into the hallway.

Julius stared after them for a moment, then burst out laughing. I put my arm through his, and with both of us chuckling, I led him to our bedroom for a little business of our own.

# Chapter 27

"SHE SAID IT'S on the View Tube," Ida May said, hovering over me as I turned on my iPad. We were in the Grind, the café I owned, and the moment we'd closed half an hour ago, Ida May had started insisting we watch Miss Kitty's TV interview. I'd finally given up and caved to her request.

"You mean YouTube?" I asked, already pulling the website up.

"YouTube? What? No. She said View Tube. A place to go watch her videos."

"Never mind," I said, already clicking on Miss Kitty's channel. "I've got it."

"Turn it up," she ordered, her eyes bright with anticipation. "It's my first interview."

"What are you talking about? You haven't been in human form since Emerson Charles zapped you back in the bayou."

"I know that. But I was there and answered some of the questions anyway. I'm hoping they caught me on camera the way Miss Kitty did while I was riding Buffy."

"This should be fun." I went to work on pouring myself a cup of coffee. It had been a long day, and one more pick-me-up couldn't hurt

The video started, and it was a close-up of Miss Kitty. She was wearing peacock feathers in her hair, a purple dress with a generous view of her assets, and a gorgeous lapis necklace. She looked more New Orleans high society than she did tiny bayou town.

"She looks fabulous," I said.

Ida May shrugged. "I suggested that outfit when she first brought up the idea of interviewing me."

I glanced at her, amused. "Of course you did."

The interview started with the questions about Miss Kitty's social media presence and quickly moved on to the gator video. Miss Kitty was animated, describing everything that had happened that day, then went on to say she'd met the ghost in question. Ida May appeared on the screen right next to Miss Kitty, her hair flying out behind her, her makeup smudged, with dark circles under her eyes, and her clothing was ripped up and covered in dirt.

"What the hell!" Ida May cried. "I don't look like that."

No, she didn't. Not ever. I peered at the screen and noted the disclaimer below the video.

*Some images may have been altered for visual entertainment.*

"Look." I pointed it out. "They changed your appearance to make you look creepy."

"This is unacceptable!" she wailed. "I take pride in my appearance. What if Sterling sees this?"

I bit my lip to keep from chuckling. "It's unlikely anyone will show it to Sterling. Being a ghost and all," I said, trying to be helpful.

"*I'm* seeing it!"

"Yeah, but—"

"Turn that trash off. I don't want to watch this anymore. What is wrong with people? Seriously, I could just—" She floated out the front door, continuing to rant to herself.

Then a few seconds later, I heard the low rumbling of a motorcycle. The one that belonged to the ghost rider, Sterling Charles. He'd taken to showing up randomly to visit with Ida May now that he was out from under Emerson's curse. Avrilla and Mia weren't the only ones who'd been controlled by the drug lord. In fact, Sterling had admitted to us that Emerson had set him up after Mia had been abducted by Emerson himself.

Sterling had just started dating her and had wanted to leave the motorcycle club, to get on the straight and narrow, but Emerson wasn't having any of it. So he'd abducted Mia to do his dirty work and pinned it on Sterling. It had worked for five years. Now Sterling was free. And he apparently was using his time to court Ida May. It was pretty sweet seeing them together actually. I liked seeing Ida May smile—something she was doing that very moment as she climbed on the back of his bike.

I put the iPad away and finished wiping down the counters. I was just about to turn the lights out and head upstairs to my apartment when I heard a key in the lock.

Jade. It was her day off. What was she doing here?

She walked in, a giant smile on her face.

"Hey you," I said, already grinning from her infections mood. "You look amazing. Did you get a facial today?"

"No. I got something, but it definitely wasn't a facial." Her eyes sparkled and her skin positively glowed.

"Then I'm going with you got laid. Not that I wanted to be thinking about that because eww, gross. None of my business, but dang you look so relaxed and—"

"Kane and I are pregnant."

Her words silenced me, and I stood there in complete shock for a second. Even though I knew they'd been trying, that was the last thing I'd expected her to say. After all the changes in my life over the past month or so, with a new dog and a brother I was responsible for, I'd completely forgotten they were trying for a child.

"Well?" she said, her smile faltering.

"Ohmigod! That's amazing. Congratulations!" I finally cried and threw my arms around her, crushing her in a bear hug. "I'm going to be an auntie!"

She laughed and hugged me back. "I just told Kane last night. We're keeping it quiet for now, but we couldn't keep this a secret from you."

I snorted. "Well, you probably could've considering I'm walking around with half a brain cell these days. Who knew teenagers and dogs could be so exhausting?"

She shook her head, a tiny smile on her lips. "You're loving every minute of it."

It was true; I was and wouldn't change any of it. "You might be right."

"I am. No doubt about it."

I eyed her, my gaze traveling over the emerald-and-diamond wedding band, her belly that wasn't even remotely showing yet, her radiant skin, and the secret smile tugging at her lips. I wanted that. All of it. And it suddenly hit me hard. An ache so intense it nearly brought tears to my eyes took up residence just over my heart. I averted my gaze and prayed she wasn't tapped into my emotions. The last thing I wanted to do was make her moment about me.

But it was too late. She placed her hand over mine and whispered, "Your time is coming, my friend. Sooner than you think."

"What?" I jerked my head back in her direction, staring her down. "Do you know something I don't?"

She gave me a coy look, then shook her head. "No. Just a feeling." Not waiting for me to answer, waved, and headed for the door.

"You're leaving already?" I asked.

She glanced back at me. "Yep. You have plans." Pointing up toward the ceiling, she added, "Julius is waiting."

The door chimed as she slipped through, leaving me by myself and wondering why Jade thought had I plans with Julius when I didn't remember making any. Was tonight the night? Had Julius clued her in on a marriage proposal? Were Julius and I ready for that? Happiness filled my soul, and I felt myself start to melt at the thought of spending the rest of my life with him.

But I quickly squashed the thought. It was too soon for promises of forever, wasn't it? We hadn't even been dating for more than three months. He must've been up to something else. A surprise dinner or a night on the town. Not champagne and diamonds.

Still, a thread of hope hung on. And a girl couldn't be blamed for wanting someone like Julius.

After locking the door and turning the lights out, I steeled myself and headed for the stairs.

When I got to my door I paused, trying to calm my breathing. My pulse was doing double time, and the anticipation was almost too much to bear. Would tonight be the start of the rest of my life?

There was only one way to find out.

I took a deep breath and walked into my apartment.

My world narrowed to nothing but Julius as my heart all but stopped.

He was in the middle of my candlelit apartment, kneeling on one knee, a ring in one hand. Smiling up at me, he gestured for me to join him. Trembling, I closed the door and somehow made my way to him.

"It's okay, Pyper," he whispered up at me. "There's no need to cry."

I was crying? I hadn't even noticed. I smiled down at him. "Must be happy tears."

A huge grin spread across his face as he took my left hand and slowly slid the art-deco-style diamond ring on my finger. "Pyper Rayne, will you do me the honor of being my wife?"

I stared at the glittering diamond, heard my earlier thoughts of *it's too soon, we should wait, no one gets married after three months.* But when I opened my mouth, only one word came out.

"Yes."

# Deanna's Book list:

## Pyper Rayne Novels
Spirits, Stilettos, and a Silver Bustier
Spirits, Rock Stars, and a Midnight Chocolate Bar
Spirits, Beignets, and a Bayou Biker Gang
Spirits, Diamonds, and a Drive-Thru Daiquiri Barn

## Jade Calhoun Novels
Haunted on Bourbon Street
Witched of Bourbon Street
Demons of Bourbon Street
Angels of Bourbon Street
Shadows of Bourbon Street
Incubus of Bourbon Street
Bewitched on Bourbon Street
Hexed on Bourbon Street

## Crescent City Fae Novels
Influential Magic
Irresistible Magic
Intoxicating Magic

## Destiny Novels
Defining Destiny
Accepting Fate

# About Deanna

New York Times and USA Today bestselling author, Deanna Chase, is a native Californian, transplanted to the slower paced lifestyle of southeastern Louisiana. When she isn't writing, she is often goofing off with her husband in New Orleans, playing with her two shih tzu dogs, or making glass beads. For more information and updates on newest releases visit her website at deannachase.com.

51471525R00140

Made in the USA
San Bernardino, CA
23 July 2017